William H. Snowden

Some Old Historic Landmarks of Virginia and Maryland

described in a hand-book for the tourist over the Washington, Alexandria

and Mount Vernon Electric Railway

William H. Snowden

Some Old Historic Landmarks of Virginia and Maryland
described in a hand-book for the tourist over the Washington, Alexandria and Mount Vernon Electric Railway

ISBN/EAN: 9783337287665

Printed in Europe, USA, Canada, Australia, Japan

Cover: Foto ©Andreas Hilbeck / pixelio.de

More available books at **www.hansebooks.com**

SOME

OLD HISTORIC LANDMARKS

OF

VIRGINIA AND MARYLAND

DESCRIBED IN

A HAND-BOOK FOR THE TOURIST

OVER THE

WASHINGTON, ALEXANDRIA AND MOUNT VERNON ELECTRIC RAILWAY.

BY

W. H. SNOWDEN,

OF ANDALUSIA, VA.

ILLUSTRATED.

PHILADELPHIA:
PRINTED BY J. B. LIPPINCOTT COMPANY.
1894.

TO THE READER.

THIS hand-book was prepared especially for tourists over the New Electric Railway from the National Capital, by way of Alexandria, to Mount Vernon. In it will be found not only a summary of the life, services, and character of General Washington, and a description of his home, his farms, and his farming operations, and the changes which have been incident to his land estate since his passing away, but also descriptions of numerous other outlying historic landmarks on both shores of the Potomac. The writer trusts that the book, hastily prepared in brief intervals of pressing duties, may prove an acceptable companion to all strangers wayfaring among the many interesting historic points which will be opened to them by this convenient and delightful route of travel to the home and tomb of the venerated Washington.

To Dr. J. M. Toner, of Washington City, the successful editor and publisher of Washington journals, diaries, and other papers; to Mr. Hubert Snowden, of the *Alexandria Gazette;* Mr. H. Harrison Dodge, the courteous and capable superintendent of Mount Vernon; Mr. J. R. C. Lewis, of Berryville, Virginia; Mr. William F. Carne, Mr. Lawrence Washington, Mrs. Dr. William Powell, and Miss Mary Lloyd, of Alexandria; Rev. M. L. Poffenberg, of Broad Creek Church; Miss Whittingham, of Baltimore, and others, the writer hereby acknowledges his obligations for valuable assistance. Should any historic reader find in the book inaccuracies, or wish to suggest additions of new facts pertaining to any of the " landmarks," they will be gratefully received for a subsequent edition.

W. H. S.

ANDALUSIA,
ARCTURUS, P. O.,
FAIRFAX CO., VA.

SOME

OLD HISTORIC LANDMARKS

OF

VIRGINIA AND MARYLAND.

ALEXANDRIA, VIRGINIA.

SEVEN miles below the National Capital, on the opposite shore of the Potomac River, stands the city of Alexandria, with a population of eighteen thousand, and a history dating back to the year 1748, when Thomas, Lord Fairfax, Lawrence Washington, and their associates, as incorporators by authority of the General Assembly of Virginia, organized the beginning of its municipal government. Fifty years before that time not a single white man had permanent residence there, and only a few years before, 1669, the whole of the domain from Great Hunting Creek to the falls of the Potomac, extending miles inland and embracing six thousand acres, had been purchased of the Indians for six hogsheads of tobacco. Within the limits of this town have occurred many noteworthy events of much more than local interest connected with our national, civil, and military records, only a few of which, however, can have even slight mention in a hand-book of travel. Here, in 1755, came Commodore Keppel, with his English naval fleet, bringing in fourteen transports, an army commanded by Major-General Edward Braddock to commence, in co-operation with the provincial forces, that memorable expedition against the French and Indians in the Ohio Valley, which ended so disastrously to the command and so fatally to their obstinate and despotic commander. The old stone building—Carlyle House—on Fairfax Street is still standing, where Braddock, Keppel, and the five provincial governors, Shirley, of Massachusetts ; Delancey, of New York ; Morris, of Pennsylvania ; Sharpe, of Maryland, and Dinwiddie, of Virginia, held a council of war in April to determine plans for the prospective campaign.

Alexandria at the opening of the present century was a prosperous commercial port, and many of her citizens acquired great wealth from traffic, and built for those times stately dwellings, the most of which still remain as fine examples of colonial architecture. Under the

5

hospitable roofs of numbers of them, still pointed out, Washington and many of his illustrious compeers of ante- and post-Revolutionary days were frequent guests.

The circumstances of the civil strife brought to this old town years of continuous excitement. Its accustomed peace and quiet were broken by the strange note and din of martial preparation, the tramp of regiments, the clatter of hurrying cavalry, and the rumble of artillery and commissary wagons and ambulances. The Ellsworth tragedy of 1861 was an event which, more than any other of that memorable time, served to widen the breach of fraternal feeling between the North and the South. The following graphic account of the occurrence is from the *Alexandria Gazette*, Industrial Edition:

" Probably no survivor of the Army of the Potomac visits Alexandria without inquiring for the Marshall House.' It became famous in history in the early days of the late war, and has so remained ever since. It was in this building that one of the bloodiest tragedies of the war was enacted, in which two men met their death in a terrible encounter.

"The spring of 1861 found Alexandria, as well as many other Southern cities, in a ferment of excitement. The place was held by a few companies of Confederate soldiers, who flaunted the stars and bars literally within sight of the Capitol and under the guns of the Federal steamer ' Pawnee,' which was anchored off the city at the time.

" One beautiful Saturday afternoon, a few weeks before the lamentable tragedy which concentrated the attention of the country on Alexandria, James Jackson, who was the lessee of the Marshall House, a sort of tavern, more than a hotel, situated on the southeast corner of King and Pitt Streets, flung to the breeze, from the roof of that building, a large-sized Confederate flag, with the defiant assertion that the man who lowered it would do so over his dead body. The occasion was one of some rejoicing and enthusiasm among those who had cast their fortunes with the Confederacy, or who sympathized with the disunion movement.

" A few days before the capture of Alexandria, President Lincoln and his Cabinet from some elevated spot in Washington, with field-glasses, viewed the objectionable flag, and in the course of the conversation that followed Mr. Lincoln remarked that the ensign of treason would not remain there long; nor did it, as on the night of Thursday, May 23, 1861, a silent move was made on this defiant city, which resulted in its capture and the stampede of its Confederate garrison to Manassas Junction, on the Orange and Alexandria (now Virginia Midland) Railroad, about twenty-seven miles distant.

" The plans of the Federal troops, through some miscarriage, proved ineffectual so far as capturing the rebel soldiers was concerned, and only a small company was netted. The Federal troops were sent in three directions when the move on the city was made—some by way of Chain Bridge above Georgetown, others *via* the Long Bridge, where trains now pass from Washington into Virginia, and the remainder by water. The Confederate pickets around the wharves and on the outskirts of the city gave the alarm in time to allow a safe retreat, and when Uncle Sam's soldiers entered the city those of the Confederacy were well on their way south.

"The New York Fire Zouaves were among those who reached Alexandria by water. No doubt their young and patriotic, though ill-starred colonel had viewed the obnoxious flag from a distance as well as Mr. Lincoln, and had longed for the opportunity of lowering it. The Marshall House is situated five blocks in a westerly direction from the wharf where the Zouaves landed. It was very early in the morning when Colonel Ellsworth, with a small squad of his men, proceeded up the streets of Alexandria, little dreaming that in less than half an hour's time his lifeless body was to be borne over the same street to the boat from which he had just landed. Cameron Street, a commercial thoroughfare, up which he wended his way, was comparatively deserted. But few people were moving, the bulk of the city's inhabitants being asleep. The inmates of the Marshall House were still in the arms of Morpheus, oblivious to the fact that the rebels had vanished before the defenders of the Union, while the flag of the Confederacy was hanging limp in the absence of any breeze. The ill-fated Colonel Ellsworth soon reached the fatal tavern and with his half-dozen followers obtained an entrance. Meeting with no opposition, and not dreaming for a moment they would encounter any resistance in the face of the fact that the city had been captured, the colonel proceeded immediately to the roof for the purpose of taking possession of the coveted flag.

"After passing through the front door, a staircase was encountered which ran spirally, the first turn leading to the second floor, the third to the next floor, and the fourth to the garret and roof. The colonel and his men, before they reached the roof, met a man in his night-clothes coming out of one of the rooms, of whom they inquired for the proprietor. The man replied that he was a boarder himself, and knew nothing of the whereabouts of the proprietor. It has since been suggested that the unknown individual was Jackson himself. It took the Zouaves but a few minutes to lower the flag and detach it from the pole which protruded from the trap-door, and Colonel Ellsworth having taken it in charge began his descent. About half-way down the flight of stairs leading from the garret he saw Jackson, but partially dressed, emerge from one of the rooms on the landing armed with a double-barrelled gun. Ellsworth, little dreaming of the bellicose nature of the man with whom he had to deal, pleasantly remarked to him, ' I've gotten a prize.' Jackson made some defiant retort, and, before any one could divine his intention, raised his gun and discharged it at the colonel. An extraordinary charge of buckshot had been placed in the weapon, and a hole was torn in the unfortunate Ellsworth's breast large enough in which to place one's fist. Colonel Ellsworth, it is said by some, fell without a groan, though others have asserted that he gave vent to an audible sigh. In his descent he fell on his face on the landing, and while his life's blood was flowing, his followers were avenging his death. The weapon Jackson used was an ordinary double-barrelled shotgun, and after killing Ellsworth he took aim at those who were with him, but before he could pull trigger the second time the gun was knocked upward by the Zouaves and the charge entered a door-frame. Francis E. Brownell, one of the squad, then sent a ball crashing into Jackson's head, and as he fell, sword-bayonets were thrust through him. Jackson's body was forced down the flight of stairs leading to the second floor and fell on the landing. The body of Ellsworth was subsequently raised by those who had accompanied him into the fatal building, covered with an American flag, and silently and sorrowfully borne to the boat from which he had a short time before landed.

"Considering the terrible tragedy which had been enacted, the day proved a remarkably quiet one. Jackson's body was soon picked up by his friends, washed, and placed in a coffin, and it lay in state throughout that day and night.

"The scene of the tragedy was visited by numbers during the day. The landing upon which Jackson fell and where he had writhed in death agony presented a sickening sight. Blood filled a space about two yards square, and it was necessary to walk upon tiptoe to avoid treading in it. There was a pool of blood about a foot square where Ellsworth had fallen.

"Colonel Farnham succeeded Ellsworth in command of the Zouaves. On the 21st of July following, the regiment participated in what proved to the Federal army the inglorious battle of Bull Run. The Zouaves and the famous Black Horse Cavalry engaged in hand-to-hand encounter throughout that eventful day, with terrible carnage to both, during which Colonel Farnham was struck on the ear by a piece of a shell, from the effect of which he died a few weeks later. In the stampede from the fatal field the Zouaves suffered greatly, and the Monday following the survivors straggled into Alexandria in a bedraggled, dejected condition, many of their comrades being then stark and stiff on the bloody field of Bull Run. A cold rain had set in, and no provisions had been made for their reception, and they were on the verge of suffering. It was in this emergency that numbers of the prominent people of Alexandria, though Southern sympathizers, exhibited a Christian spirit which the good-natured Zouaves were not slow to appreciate. Houses were opened and entertainment afforded many of them and their straggling *confrères* by parties whose political predilections were hostile to the principles for which the vanquished had fought.

"The Zouaves lingered about Alexandria for a few months, and, the term of their enlistment having expired, they were mustered out of service.

"Jackson, the destroyer of Colonel Ellsworth, was a typical Southerner. Though brave and fearless, his political predilections had run riot with his judgment, and, rather than let the rash threat of protecting his flag come to naught, he preferred sacrificing his life. There is little to be said in palliation of his act save that he lived at a time when men's blood had reached the fever-heat of excitement, and when rashness was occasionally exhibited by the champions of both sides.

"The killing of Ellsworth produced the greatest sorrow as well as exasperation at the North, and Alexandria was immediately besieged by

CHRIST CHURCH, ALEXANDRIA, VA.

(Page 6.)

MARSHALL HOUSE.

(Page ...)

LAFAYETTE HOUSE.

(Page ...)

parties from a distance anxious to inspect the scene of the tragedy. A piece of oil-cloth on the landing on which the colonel fell was gradually cut up and carried away by relic hunters. The flooring subsequently met the same fate, and finally the balusters were cut away, piece by piece, and carried North. For several years the old Marshall House was looked upon as a sad memento of war times by soldiers of both sides—by the Federals as the place where a brave and promising young officer laid down his life at the beginning of the four-years' conflict, and by the Confederates as the spot where a determined sympathizer of their cause showed a courage in the face of inevitable death equalled by few on either side.

"About seventeen years ago, on a cold, weird night, the Marshall House was found to be on fire, and, despite the exertions of the fire department, but little more than the bare walls were left standing. Upon being rebuilt, it ceased to be a house of entertainment, and the new building is used for other purposes."

There is more at Alexandria to call up the memory of Washington than in any other place in our country except that of Mount Vernon. Alexandria was, emphatically, his own town. It was his post-office, his voting- and market-place. It was the meeting-place of the lodge of Freemasons to which he belonged. He was a member of its corporation council, and owned property within its limits. He was the commander of its local militia, and was a member of its volunteer fire company. He slept in the houses of many of its leading citizens, and danced the minuet with its fairest daughters. He was a vestryman of the parish, and was a regular attendant of Christ Church, where his pew is kept undisturbed to this day. The tourist who enters Alexandria by way of the Pennsylvania Railroad and takes the city electric railway at the head of Cameron Street will find Christ Church at the corner of that and Washington Street, four squares from the local dépôt. On the greensward of this church, seen on the left as the car turns from Cameron into Columbus Street, Washington, in 1774, first counselled resistance to British tyranny. There, too, in 1861, General Lee first agreed to take command of the Virginia forces at the opening of the Civil War. Continuing and turning into King Street the car crosses Washington Street, where looking to the right may be seen the Confederate monument at the place where the Alexandria soldiers left for the war, May 24, 1861. Two blocks further east at Pitt Street the car reaches the Marshall House, on the right hand side, noted for the meeting and tragic death of Colonel Elmer Ellsworth and Captain James Jackson. The east window of the second story marks the place of the encounter. At this part of the street in early days were the head springs of Orinoco Creek, which one hundred yards north washed the foot of a hill on which stood Washington's town house, which, from 1763 to 1799, whenever he came up from Mount Vernon, he used for the transaction of business. Then passing still further to the east the car at Royal Street reaches the point where, the house on the northwest corner being afire, Washington leaped from his horse and assisted to work the old Friendship engine. Look a hundred feet north and see on the west side the City

Hotel, from the door of which, in 1799, Washington gave his last military order to the Alexandria volunteers. On the east side see now, surmounted by a tower, the market-house which covers the spot where Washington had his encounter with Colonel Payne, so familiar to historic students. Here, also, is a museum in connection with the Masonic lodge, of which Washington was a member, containing many relics and mementos of the past, and particularly of the *pater patriæ*. At the next block where the cars turn into Fairfax Street, note at the turn on the left the old frame, hip-roofed house, built in 1763, as the mansion of Colonel William Ramsay, a connection of Washington, and where the great chief was a frequent visitor. One hundred yards north, up Fairfax Street, stands within the area of the Braddock House the stone building, residence of John Carlyle, where the governors of the provinces, before mentioned, held with Braddock and Keppel their council of war.

The visit of General Lafayette to Alexandria is one of the green spots in the city's history. There are some now living who remember the occasion; others who have a dim recollection of it when, as little children, they toddled along, having hold of their parents' hands. This was in the year 1824. The city at that time put on a holiday attire, and the enthusiasm animated all from the youngest to the oldest.

At that time hundreds of Alexandrians could be found who had fought through the seven years' conflict for independence. To them the name of Lafayette was sacred. and many who participated in the honors conferred upon the illustrious Frenchman had been encouraged by his presence and valor on the field of battle.

It is unnecessary to describe all the details of his reception and entertainment while here. Let it suffice when it is said that almost every one in the community turned out and vied in doing honor to him who, when the infant republic most needed help, left his own land and cast his fortune with us, and lived to see the independence of a country declared which has grown and prospered ever since.

The house where Lafayette was entertained while in Alexandria is one of the most prominent in the city. It is situated on the southwest corner of St. Asaph and Duke Streets, and is now occupied by Mrs. Susan C. Smoot. Such are a few of the many points of historic interest which the old town possesses for the curious wayfarer within its borders.

FROM ALEXANDRIA TO MOUNT VERNON.

MOUNT VERNON, the home and last resting-place of George Washington, the illustrious commander-in-chief of our colonial armies, and the first President of the United States, is distant from Alexandria nine miles, and is most conveniently reached by the comfortable cars of the new electric railway, a road which, for thoroughness in construction, equipment, service, and safety, is not surpassed by any other in the United States. Its course lies down the Virginia shore of the Potomac and through a region of country abounding in

BRADDOCK'S HEADQUARTERS, ALEXANDRIA, VA.

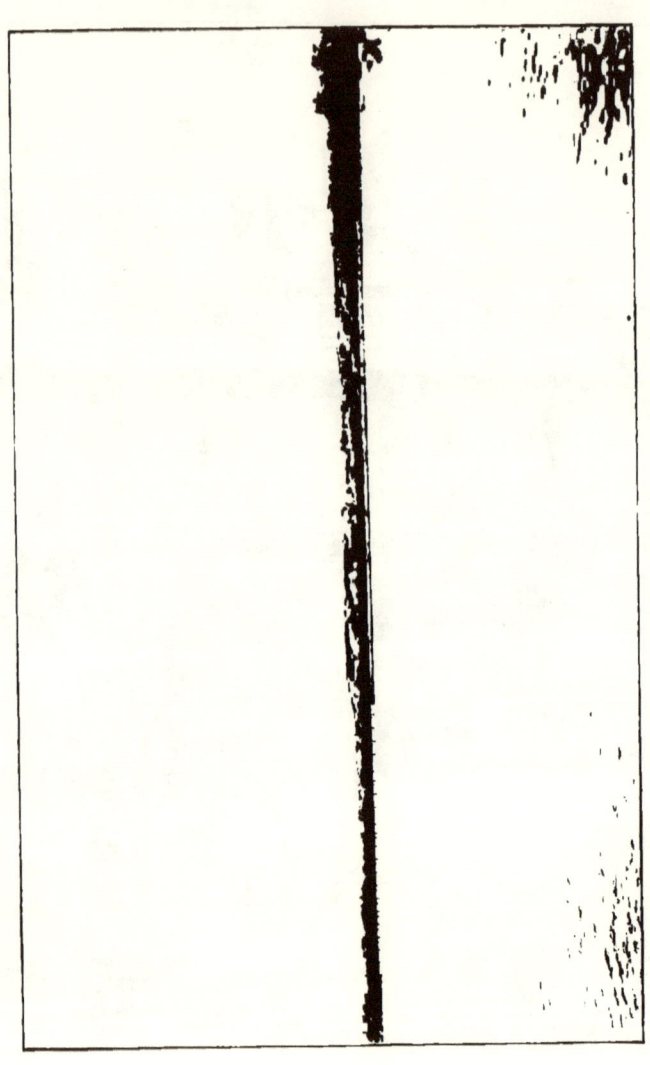

SEMINARY RIDGE AND EARLY PICKETING GROUNDS, FROM ELECTRIC RAILWAY BRIDGE.

attractive natural scenery and interesting historic associations, and the run is made in half an hour at frequent intervals every day.

Emerging from Alexandria by way of Fairfax Street, a very pleasing view of the Potomac, with its broad estuary of Great Hunting Creek, is presented to the eye. Immediately to the left is Light House Point, which marked the southeastern boundary corner of the old Virginia limits of the District of Columbia, as they were run and established in 1791. Opposite, on the Maryland shore, are seen Rozier's Bluff and the heights of Fort Foote; and further down the expanse of Broad Bay uniting with the Potomac. To the right, looking from the railway bridge over Hunting Creek, stretches a scope of country pleasingly diversified by gently sloping hills and vales, and dotted with hamlet and farm-houses. Prominent among the many objects of the landscape is the tall spire of the Episcopal Theological Seminary, which, if it could speak of the transactions of some of the years of the past, could tell startling stories of the presence of mustering armies. Around it in almost every direction, at the beginning of the civil strife, the plains and hill slopes were white with the tents of the gathered regiments, brigades, and divisions of Union soldiers. Everywhere over the suddenly populated region was heard the drum's wild beats, the fife's shrill notes, the bugle's echoing calls. The numerous remains of their intrenchments, earthworks, and other defences still prominent at every turn for miles, attest with melancholy certainty the great preparations which were then made by them for the impending conflict, which ere long broke with such terrific force within our borders. Union forts frowned from every salient point of those now so quiet and peaceful hills, and a hundred flagstaffs unfurled over all, their starry flags to the passing winds. The locality is one naturally possessing a saddening interest to the tourist. Every year it is visited by numbers of the surviving veterans who figured in the scenes of its stirring times of over thirty years ago.

Just beyond the Seminary, in full sight up the valley, are the picketing grounds which long divided the two armies; and near by is Bailey's Cross Roads, where was manœuvred by the Union forces one of the grandest military reviews of any country or time. Through these camping and drilling grounds, and far on beyond, may still be traced the course of the old military road, laid out through the then dense wilderness a hundred years previous, by which a portion of Braddock's army under General Halket marched on their disastrous expedition.

Fairfax Court House, from the Seminary, is distant fourteen miles, and the battle-field of Bull Run about twenty. Half-way between the Seminary and the railway bridge is Cameron Ford, where Hunting Creek is crossed by the old highway from Alexandria to Fredericksburg and Richmond. Over this highway, less than a hundred years before, one bright morning in the month of August, three horsemen starting from Mount Vernon might have been seen pursuing their journey to Philadelphia to attend the first session of the General Continental Congress, which was to commence on the fifth of the September following. They were George Washington, Patrick Henry, and Edmund

Pendleton, all of Virginia—truly a noble companionship. Washington in the meridian of his days, mature in wisdom, comprehensive in mind, sagacious in foresight. Henry in the youthful vigor and elasticity of his bounding genius; ardent, acute, fanciful, eloquent. Pendleton, schooled in public life, a veteran in council, with native force of intellect, and habits of deep reflection. Such were these apostles of liberty repairing on their august pilgrimage to the Quaker City to assist in laying the foundations of a mighty empire.

Over this highway, too, General Sherman in 1865 led his army back to the National Capital on their return from marching from "Atlanta to the sea." Over this same highway, too, Washington always passed when he rode into Alexandria on horseback or in his coach. It was also in colonial and long-after times the great thoroughfare of all the Southern Atlantic seaboard travel to Philadelphia, New York, Boston, and other Northern cities. Then it was not so easy a matter for the members of Congress to get to the "sessions" as at present. The transit from California to New York is now made in less time by flying train than was then required to make the old stage-coach journey from Richmond to the same city. A short distance above the railway bridge is the new iron bridge of the turnpike to Accotink, ten miles distant, and just beyond on the hill crest to the right are the almost intact earthworks of Fort Lyons, the most southerly and the strongest of the sixty-eight inclosed forts and batteries of that long cordon of war-time defences of over thirty miles in length. Nearby Fort Lyons is Mount Eagle. Here was the home, still remaining, of Brian, seventh Lord Fairfax and son of William of Belvoir. He was rector of Christ Church, Alexandria, from 1790 to 1792. His title was confirmed to him by the House of Lords in 1800. Mount Eagle was on the road over which Washington always passed going to Alexandria, and he was a frequent visitor there.

Leaving the bridge of Hunting Creek the railway enters next and passes through the lands of the "New Alexandria Land and River Improvement Company." Their town, projected two years ago, already numbers two factories, a spacious hotel, and a number of neat cottages—a nucleus which will no doubt be, ere long, rapidly augmented with the revival of financial confidence throughout our country, since the company offers extraordinary inducements to manufacturers and others to come in and help to make their enterprise a success.

From New Alexandria the course of the road is along the river shore over an uninterrupted alluvial level until it reaches the station at the "Dyke," when it gradually rises by a slight deflection to the right until it ascends to the highlands at Belmont Station, still a mile farther. Beyond this station a few hundred paces is the line of survey marking the upper boundary of the "Old Mount Vernon Estate" of eight thousand acres, which in Washington's time was divided into five main farms or plantations, and designated respectively, River, Dogue Run, Mansion House, Union, and Muddy Hole farms. River farm, which the railway strikes first, and formerly known as Clifton's Neck, was purchased in 1760 for the sum of three dollars per acre. It consisted of two thousand acres, but has been since divided and

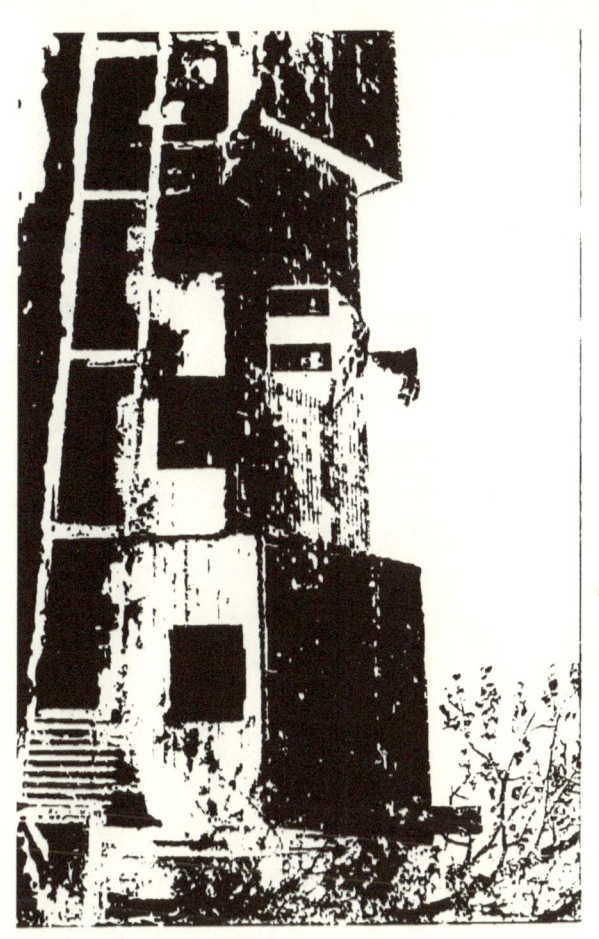

MOUNT EAGLE, NEAR ALEXANDRIA, VA.

Home of Brian, Seventh Lord Fairfax.

WELLINGTON HOUSE.
Home of Washington's Private Secretary.

subdivided like all the other farms into smaller tracts, and are occupied by settlers chiefly from the Northern States of New Jersey, Pennsylvania, New York, and elsewhere, who have made many improvements upon them by clearing up the grounds, enriching the soil, planting orchards, and constructing fencing and comfortable dwellings. The surface of these highlands is gently undulating, and consists of a great diversity of soils, which are remarkably easy of tillage, and very susceptible of a high and profitable fertilization, and are particularly adapted to the production of all kinds of farm staples, fruits, and garden vegetables needed by the adjacent cities. The divisions lying immediately along the river afford situations for homes of surpassing beauty; and while they are proverbially healthy, and are abundantly supplied with perennial springs of pure soft water for every domestic requirement, the railway makes them suburban by giving them quick and easy transits to and from the National Capital at all times of the year.

A short distance from Wellington Station to the left and in full view stands on the river-bank the old Wellington House, built by Washington in 1768. It was occupied by Colonel Tobias Lear, who was private and military secretary to the general, and afterwards private tutor to his adopted children, George W. Parke Custis, and his sister Nelly, and who was in 1805 United States commissioner to treat with the hostile powers of the Barbary states at the time of the memorable expedition of General Eaton. By a provision of Washington's will he was to be tenant of the house and premises rent free until his death. This was in consideration of his great services to him, and especially during the war. He died in 1816. Afterwards, the farm was occupied by two generations of the Washington family, Charles A., a grand-nephew, being the last, until 1859. Charles was a genial, jolly fellow, but not so well up in the arts of practical farming as his illustrious uncle. On one occasion, he went into town to have some ploughshares sharpened which were urgently needed to make ready his grounds for wheat sowing, but falling in with some old cronies he was induced to make a month's visit to the " Springs ;" but it was all the same to Uncle Toby and the rest of the waiting " hands," for they had a long holiday, though the wheat crop went by default. In farming he was an experimentalist, though always disastrously. He read in the *Country Gentleman* of the great profits of barley growing, and so resolved to try his hand also. One morning in spring, when the robin and bluebird were piping their jubilant songs, he had his "gang" ploughing a ten-acre field. The barley was sown, and the harvest time came, and the grain was flailed out and loaded on a two-horse team for the Alexandria market. The hopeful proprietor mounted his saddle-horse and rode in, in advance to dispose of his crop. But barley was an unknown quantity he found, on arriving at the store of his merchants; but later, however, he succeeded in bartering his grains to a brewer for a barrel of beer, which he sent home to his cellar. The tidings of the transaction soon spread among his many jolly town companions, and, slipping down the river by boat after nightfall to the Wellington House, they succeeded before morning in drinking up the entire crop of barley.

From Arcturus, the next station beyond, a smooth, winding avenue leads down a few hundred paces to Andalusia, one of the many desirable places on the "Old Estate" which the railway has made readily accessible to those who are in quest of situations for charming suburban homes. This point in our journey is best described in the subjoined story of "A Summer Outing."

THE STORY OF AN OUTING AT ANDALUSIA, VA.

TWELVE miles from the National Capital, down the Potomac on the Virginia shore, is a spot whose memories will be like holy benedictions to me through all the coming years of my life. I was needing rest, and there I found it in a sweet and quiet seclusion such as I had never enjoyed before,—a rest which had no circumstance to disturb nor shadow to mar.

This place Elysian is reached by the Mount Vernon Electric Railway. From Arcturus Station, midway between Alexandria and the home of Washington, you wind by a hard, smooth avenue along green fields, and through orchards laden with ripe and ripening fruitage, till you are within the cooling shadows of a hundred stately oaks and walnuts, many of them of a century's growth. Here in the midst of these leafy sentinels is a home which in all its surroundings and influences, more nearly than any other, fills up the measure of my ideal dreamings.

Andalusia is distant from the travelled highways, and before the coming of the electric car was a *terra incognita*, with rarely a visitor, save from the surrounding neighborhood, to invade its quiet borders. The passenger from the deck of the passing steamer descried it in the distance, showing like a gem in its setting of river and cool embowering trees, but it was only a glimpse of hidden beauties to be remembered and cherished or forgotten. Now by rapid and easy transit many pilgrims find their way thither, although it is but a private home. Little picnic parties from the cities adjacent, through the courtesy of the proprietor, hie there through the summer days to spread their repasts under the shadowing boughs, and make merry on the inviting green sward. Artists come to sketch the delightful and varied views of its environs, the cycler to wheel over the smooth avenues, the angler to throw his line into the still river nooks, and the wearied, like myself, to seek the balm of rest.

In this ideal home by the Potomac I found a welcome and a hospitality which recalled the many stories I had read, of entertainments in Virginia homes of the olden time. For tired nature there was no lack of sweet restorers. There were libraries, inviting to every range and department of knowledge. There was music to soothe and harmonize, pictures, and cabinets of curios to amuse, and a wilderness of flowers to please the eye.

All too swiftly passed the time, as I fondly tarried in the midst of so many allurements from the dull and perplexing routine of business in the city. Hours of the bright midsummer days I watched from the vine-hung verandas of the "Old Mansion," the broad river's

VIEW UP THE POTOMAC, LOOKING FROM ANDALUSIA.

expanse before me, with its flitting cloud shadows, its sails, and passing steamers. Sometimes it was a leisure stroll along the pebbly shore, or boating in the still waters that beguiled me, and sometimes it was straying over the site of the old Indian town of Assaomeck, looking for arrow-heads, javelin points, fragments of pottery, and other remains of the ancient dwellers.

One serene evening, as the parting rays of the setting sun were fading beyond the hills I joined a boating party for an excursion to the opposite shores of "Maryland, my Maryland." A delightful ride over a stretch of two miles of the still waters brought us to the head of "Broad Bay," where we landed, and then walked in the twilight a short distance up the valley to an ancient chapel, erected in the time when all the surrounding region was a part of the realms which owned the rule and sway of the king of "Old England." Within the walls of this chapel, our Washington, Lord Fairfax, and many other noted men of that time were wont to worship. Many generations of its congregations are lying under the crumbling and fallen stones of its bramble-grown graveyard; and as I pondered where so often had been read that last, solemn ritual of "dust to dust," many a vision flitted before me, of happy bridals and solemn funeral trains of the "dead past" of the long ago.

As we turned in pensive mood from the sacred place, the full moon was up and beaming brightly on the still waters of the grand old river to light us back on our homeward way.

The sketch of my outing would be incomplete, if I failed to mention a sail down the river to Fort Washington, and also a ride over the electric road to Mount Vernon. Reader, did you ever climb to the heights of the old fort? If not, it is worth a journey to do so. Go there on some fair midsummer day, and survey from its vine-covered battlements the broad and varied expanse outlying before them. In that expanse the eye may trace out the National Capital, with its towering dome and obelisk, sitting superbly enthroned in the mist and dimness of the far away hills to the north; and the grand old river flowing down in its seaward course through its setting of green slopes and plains and wooded crests gives to all the view a charm and beauty not often surpassed.

A visit to the home and tomb of the immortal chieftain is surely an event to linger long in the memory of every patriot.

But I am reaching the limits of the typos, so must not linger, otherwise the story of my outing with its round of varied pleasures and enjoyments would be a long one. To the friends who had kindly bidden and welcomed me to their hospitalities I said good-by, and with many regrets at parting turned homeward from the long to be remembered scenes of Andalusia.

From Andalusia to Mount Vernon the distance is four miles, with the intervening stations of Herbert's Spring, Snowden, Hunter's, and Riverside Park at Little Hunting Creek, which make the occupants of numerous adjacent farms conveniently accessible to this important line of travel. The creek divides the Original River Farm of Washington's map from the Mansion House Farm, and one mile beyond the road terminates at the gates of the Mount Vernon Mansion.

BROAD CREEK—OLD CHURCH AND OLD HOUSES.

FOUR miles below Alexandria, on the Maryland shore, and opposite to Andalusia, on the Virginia side, is the estuary or bay of Broad Creek. There Washington often went, as he tells us in his diary, with his friend and neighbor, Diggs, of Warburton Manor, to throw his line for the finny denizens of the still waters. At the head of this bay, where now only the light-draught scow-boat can ascend the silt-filled channel, large schooners used to lie at their moorings and load with cargoes of tobacco, wheat, and corn for foreign ports. It was a busy neighborhood then, when the odd and ancient-looking houses, which have stood through the changes of one hundred and fifty to two hundred years, were comparatively new, and the surrounding lands were fertile and produced abundantly all kinds of farm products.

There is much in this isolated locality to interest the curious delver into the scenes and circumstances of the olden time. The weather-beaten tenements, so dilapidated and forlorn in appearance; the impoverished fields and the forsaken landing-place, with never a freight or cargo to be loaded or discharged, will murmur to him, as he thoughtfully scans the desolation, in audible stories of how the generations of toilers came and went—how they fretted out life's fitful fever, and were at last gathered from their labors of success or failure to the densely populated burial-place of the settlement.

More than two hundred years ago an Episcopal church was organized here by the first dwellers. The parish was at first known as Piscataway, afterwards King George's, and the Church of St. John's. The first house for worship was of logs and built in 1694, rebuilt with bricks in 1722, and enlarged to its present dimensions in 1763. John Addison, William Hatton, William Hutchinson, William Tannhill, John Emmet, and John Smallwell were of its first vestry, and Rev. George Tubman its first rector. This church antedates all other Episcopal churches of the Potomac region of Maryland. The burial-place of the old kirk is densely peopled with the dead of departed congregations. Over most of the graves is a wilderness of tangled vines. Many of the stones are levelled and sunken nearly out of sight, with inscriptions worn and hard to decipher. Hundreds of graves have no stones at all, presumably of the earliest burials. A broad marble slab lies over the remains of Enoch Lyells, killed in a duel, August 7, 1805, with the following inscription :

> Go, our dear son, obey the call of Heaven;
> Thy sins were few—we trust they are forgiven.
> Yet, oh, what pen can paint the parents' woe?
> God only can punish the hand that gave the blow.

The quarrel of the duelists had its origin in offensive remarks made at a ball in the village of Piscataway, and the duel took place at Johnson's Spring, on the Virginia shore. The young man who was killed and who had made the remarks was averse to the encounter, but was goaded on to his death by his father and mother. His antagonist was named Bowie.

ACROSS THE RIVER TO BROAD BAY, FROM ANDALUSIA.

OLD HOUSE AT BROAD CREEK, MD.
200 years old.

ST. JOHN'S CHURCH, BROAD CREEK, MD.
200 years old.

(Page 16.)

THE DOGUE INDIANS—ASSAOMECK.

Alas for them ! their day is o'er,
Their fires are out from shore to shore ;
No more for them the wild deer bounds,—
The plough is on their hunting-grounds.
The pale man's axe rings thro' their woods ;
The pale man's sail skims o'er their floods.

ON the shores of the Mount Vernon estate, and far inland to the west, once roamed a numerous tribe of aborigines whose prowess was acknowledged and feared by all the surrounding tribes. The chief settlement or village of "Assaomeck," according to the investigations of Professor Holmes, of the National Ethnological Bureau, occupied the site now known as Andalusia, four miles below Alexandria. The great numbers of stone axes, javelin and arrow points, and fragments of pottery which have been turned up there by the plough, sufficiently attest the fact. Here, in 1608, that fearless explorer and doughty old soldier, Captain John Smith, on his way up the Potomac to beyond the present site of the National Capital, stopped to hold parley with the reigning chief, and smoke the pipe of peace and friendship.

FORT WASHINGTON, AND THE MOUTH OF THE PISCATAWAY—LEONARD CALVERT WITH HIS VANGUARD OF RELIGIOUS LIBERTY.

SEVEN miles below Alexandria, on the commanding heights of the old manorial estate of "Warburton," in Maryland, are the frowning battlements of Fort Washington. They help to give picturesqueness to the grand landscape of which they are a part, and they represent an expenditure of many hundred thousands of the public treasury, and many years of hard toil of long-vanished builders. But that is all. For the defence of the National Capital, they are practically useless against the new methods of naval attacks. In 1814, when the British fleet came up the Potomac, the garrison then occupying the works abandoned them and allowed the enemy to proceed to Alexandria and plunder the city without molestation. At the foot of the heights, just under the walls where the waters of the Piscataway and the Potomac unite, came, in 1634, Governor Leonard Calvert with two hundred followers, most of them Roman Catholic gentlemen and their servants, to establish, under the provisions of a royal charter to his brother, Cecil Calvert (Lord Baltimore), a settlement of the new region of Maryland, as yet untenanted save by roving aborigines. He anchored his vessels, the "Dove" and a small pinnace, and proceeded to negotiate with the Indians, who assembled on the shore to the number of five hundred. The chieftain of the tribe would neither bid him go nor stay. "He might use his own discretion." It did not seem safe for the English to plant their first settlement in the wilderness so high up the river, whereupon Calvert descended the stream, examining in his barge the creeks and estuaries near the Chesapeake. He entered the river now called St. Mary's,

2

and which he named St. George's, and "about four leagues from its
junction with the Potomac" he anchored at the Indian town of Yoa-
comoco. To Calvert the spot seemed convenient for a plantation.
Mutual promises of friendship were made between the English and the
natives, and upon the twenty-seventh day of March, 1634, the Catho-
lics took quiet possession of the place, and religious liberty obtained
a home—its only home in the wide world—at the humble village
which bore the name of St. Mary's.

GEORGE WASHINGTON AND HIS HOME.

> Tell us again the story
> Our sires and grandsires told ;
> We love to hear it often,
> 'Tis ever new, tho' old.

ON the fourteenth day of December, 1799, George Washington,
the successful soldier and leader, the true patriot, the wise statesman, the estimable private citizen, the public benefactor and friend of
all mankind, passed peacefully from earth, in his quiet home at Mount
Vernon, to the inheritance of the rich rewards awaiting a life of exceeding great usefulness and honor. Since the occurrence of that event
which brought grief and sorrow to the infant nation he had so faithfully labored to direct and establish, only ninety-five years have elapsed,
hardly five generations of his posterity ; and a few are still remaining
among us who were then children. Yet, such was the sublime character and great worth of the revered chief, and such have been the
grand results to the world of his heroic deeds and unselfish sacrifices
that, in our grateful remembrance and almost pious veneration of him,
the vista of time through which we look back in contemplation of his
life and public services seems to us more like one of long centuries
than that of the few scores of solemn anniversaries which have been
recorded. As this vista lengthens and grows dimmer with the passing
away of each succeeding year, we delight more and more to recount
the story of his childhood and early training, of his military services
and exploits, of his subsequent civil career, and, finally, of his retired
life as a farmer on his broad Virginia estate, where, in the peaceful
tranquillity of a mind untroubled by vain ambitions or harassing regrets, he lived the happiest days of his eventful life.

Mount Vernon, the home and tomb, will ever continue the grand
focal point to which the generations of our republic will fondly turn
in their love and admiration for the great chief. Then shall we not
keep on telling the "old, old story" ?—the story which, though so
often repeated, will be forever new, and will forever charm and please,
—the one which poets shall sing and orators proclaim—the one which
sires and grandsires shall relate to the eager ears of little children on
their knees, which shall cross every sea, and be heard in every land
and in every clime. Let it be told, and again and again repeated,
so that no event or circumstance connected with the brilliant career
of the *pater patriæ* shall remain unknown or forgotten. His life and
the precious memories of its well-shaped and rounded works are the
common patrimony, and will be kept fresh and perennial.

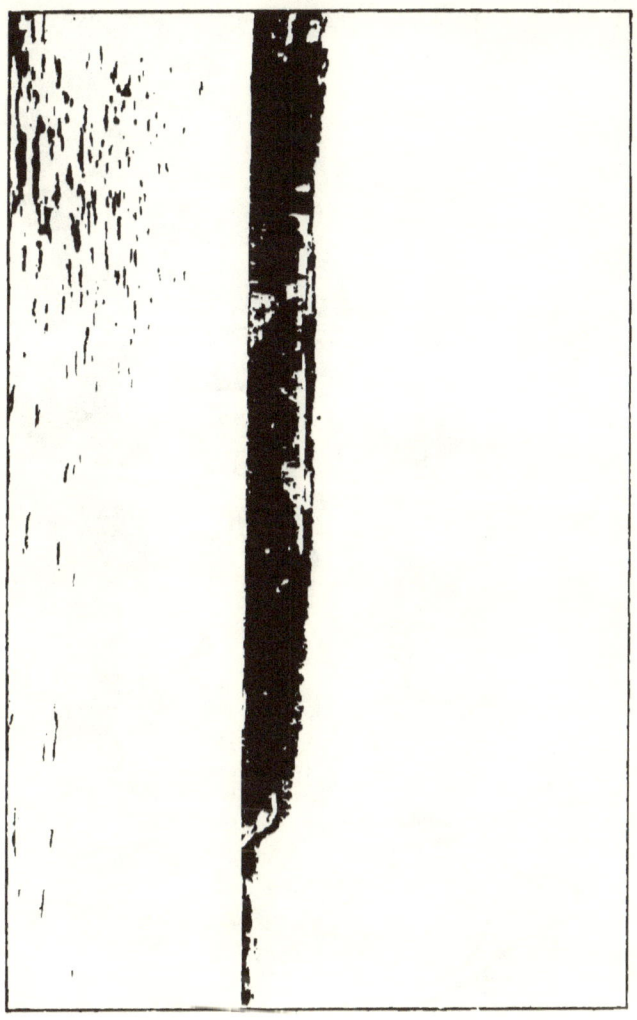

FORT WASHINGTON AND MOUTH OF PISCATAWAY RIVER.

MOUNT VERNON.

WASHINGTON'S LINEAGE—THE MOUNT VERNON HOME.

THE political dissensions which convulsed the English people in the beginning of the eighteenth century, finally brought violent death to their king, Charles the First, and established in the place of their monarchical government, the protectorate of Oliver Cromwell. As a result of the revolution, the prominent adherents of royalty found themselves without occupation or favor under the new rule, and many of them left the country and sought asylum in the newly-opened lands beyond the sea. Among this number were two brothers, John and Andrew Washington, of Yorkshire, men of note and goodly reputation in their native manor, and descended from a long and illustrious line of families whose genealogy dated back nearly to the time of the Norman conquest. Virginia was already quite numerously settled by English cavaliers, who still kept up their allegiance to monarchy and the Anglican Church. With these far-away colonists the brothers joined their influences and destinies in the year 1657, and immediately purchased of Lord Thomas Culpeper a large tract of land in the county of Westmoreland, bordering the Potomac River. John married a Miss Anna Pope of the same county, and took up his residence on Bridge's Creek. He found the lands very rich, and became an extensive planter, and shipped large quantities of tobacco to England and Holland. He was popular among the colonists, filled the office of magistrate, and served many sessions in the House of Burgesses. Possessing a spark of the old military fire of some of his ancestors, we find him, according to the records, as Colonel Washington, leading the Virginia military forces in conjunction with those of Maryland against a band of Seneca Indians, who were raiding the settlements of that region. In honor of his sterling worth and distinguished public services, the parish in which he lived was called after him, and still bears the honored name of Washington. He died January, 1677, and his remains lie entombed in the family burying-ground at Bridge's Creek. By his will a portion of his original purchase or purchases, consisting of two thousand five hundred acres lying between Dogue Run and Little Hunting Creek, now in Fairfax County, was devised to his son Lawrence, from whom it descended by will to *his* son Augustine, born 1694, by his first marriage to Jane Butler. From Augustine, who died April 12, 1743, it descended to *his* oldest son, Major Lawrence Washington, who was married to Annie, oldest daughter of William Fairfax, of Belvoir. This portion or tract of land was the nucleus of the Mount Vernon estate. On coming into possession of it, Lawrence Washington cleared and cultivated the lands and built the middle portion of the mansion, consisting of four rooms, and named the place Mount Vernon in honor of Admiral Vernon, under whom he had served as a soldier at the siege of Carthagena. He died July 26, 1752, at the age of thirty-four, and was buried in the great vault at Mount Vernon. His portrait hangs in the Mount Vernon mansion. In his will the Mount Vernon estate was devised to his daughter Sarah, with the provision that if she should die without issue it was to become the property of his "loving brother" George, which so transpired, as she survived her father but a short time, and so his brother, or half-brother as was the fact, inherited the estate, and came into full possession of it before he was twenty-one years of age. The widow of Lawrence had been amply provided for by bequests of other lands, and afterwards was married to Colonel George Lee, an uncle of Arthur and Richard Henry Lee, of Revolutionary fame and memory. Owing to his connection with the military operations at that time, by the colonists against the French and Indians on the Ohio frontier, George was absent from Mount Vernon during the most of seven years. He came to its occupancy in the year 1759, after the fall of Fort Duquesne, the defeat of the combined enemies, and the cessation of hostilities, and shortly after was married to Mrs. Martha Custis, the beautiful and wealthy widow of Colonel John Custis.

Washington was now twenty-seven years of age, in the full vigor of health, and being free from engrossing public engagements, with the exception of his duties as a member of the colonial legislature, to which he had just been elected, he steadily bent his energies and judgment to the personal management and improvement of his home on the Potomac. As already noted this consisted of a dwelling with a ground floor of four rooms and a scope of twenty-five hundred acres of land. He subsequently enlarged the dwelling-place to its present proportions, extended the boundaries of the estate, already extensive, so as to include five thousand five hundred more, with a frontage along tide water of nearly ten miles, and then commenced a series of changes over the entire area which in the course of a few years amply demonstrated to all who witnessed the results that he was as sensible and practical as a farmer as he had been in his methods of fighting the Indians. Whenever necessary he drained the grounds, adopted the plan of rotating crops, procured the best agricultural implements then to be obtained, planted and sowed the best seeds, erected comfortable shelters for his overseers and hands, had his home smithy and wagon-shops for the repairs of all tools, carts and wagons, his carpenters for building and repairing the farm buildings and fences, had his grist-mill for grinding his grains, his huntsmen for procuring wild game and his fishermen for supplying everybody on the premises with fish, then so abundant in the river. In a word, all things on the estate were so directed as to best subserve the end of making the most of all existing possibilities and satisfying all the reasonable wants of a rural community such as was there maintained. Under the vigilant eye of the distinguished master everything went on with regularity and certainty. He carefully looked after the details of his farm operations, and being a very observant man, he never in any of his journeys abroad failed to notice any new agricultural improvements, and was very ready always to put it into practice on his own acres. Bringing to his aid the knowledge he had acquired in marking out the boundaries in his younger days of the wilderness possessions of Lord Fairfax in the valley of the Shenandoah with compass and chain, he himself laid off his estate into five main farms. The portion in the elbow of the Po-

GEORGE WASHINGTON.

Received February 26.th 1765. From George Washington the
sum of Twenty five pounds Cur.y. being the consideration
money within mentioned – Pay received by me

John   his X mark   Connely
        mark

tomac, and between that stream and Little Hunting Creek, was named and known as Clifton's Neck or River Farm, being the first of the land of the Mount Vernon estate entered by the railway going down from Alexandria, and consisted of about two thousand acres. Between Little Hunting Creek were laid off the Mansion House Farm of 1200 acres, Union Farm of 1000 acres, Dogue Run Farm of 2000 acres, and Muddy Hole Farm of 1300 acres.

Several of these local names are found in Washington's will, which devises the property east of Little Hunting Creek, to George Fayette Washington ; about two-thirds of the portion between Little Hunting Creek and Dogue Creek, lying on the Potomac, and including the Mansion House Farm, to Bushrod Washington : and the residue being the southwesterly part of this tract, to Lawrence Lewis and his wife Eleanor Park Lewis. The soil and other natural capabilities of his estate are accurately described by Washington. The greater part he says is a grayish loam running to clay. Some parts of it are of a dark mould, some inclined to sand, scarcely any to stone. He adds, "A husbandman's will, could not lay the farms more level than they are." And as to the river, " the whole shore is one entire fishery," "and springs, with plenty of water for man and cattle, abound everywhere on the grounds."

In addition to his own dwelling-house and other buildings on the Mansion House Farm, he had, what he calls, an overlooker's house and negro quarters on each of the other farms. He speaks also of a newly erected brick barn, "equal, perhaps, to any in America," on the Union Farm, a new circular barn on Dogue Run Farm, and a gristmill hear the mouth of Dogue Run. Some idea of the extent of Washington's farming operations may be formed from the following facts. In 1787 he had five hundred and eighty acres in grass, four hundred acres in oats, seven hundred acres in wheat, the same number in corn, with several hundred acres in barley, buckwheat, potatoes, peas, beans, and turnips. His live stock consisted of one hundred and forty horses, one hundred and twelve cows, two hundred and twenty-six working oxen, heifers and steers, and five hundred sheep, and of hogs, many, almost numberless, running at large in the woodlands and marshes. He constantly employed two hundred and fifty hands (negroes), and kept a score of ploughs going during the entire year, when the earth and the state of the weather would permit. In 1780 he slaughtered one hundred and fifty hogs for the use of his family and negroes. When not called away from Mount Vernon by public duties, Washington rode daily over his farms in pleasant weather, and kept himself thoroughly acquainted with the details of everything that was going on from season to season over his broad acres. Every locality was mapped. Every branch of labor was systematized, and all his farming operations were in charge of competent overseers, who were required to regularly account to him of their stewardship with exactness.

With the passing away of the winter of 1799 passed also from earth the stately presence of him who gave to the home and estate of Mount Vernon all their historic character and importance, and endeared them

for all time to the generations of his countrymen to come after him;
but thenceforth for many a long year, in the absence of the tireless
care and watchful eye of the master, the fair fields were despoiled of
their wonted fertility, and abandoned afterwards to the pine and cedar
and the returning wild deer. The mansion itself and the immediate
surroundings were sadly suffering from neglect and the hands of the
spoiler.

Such was the condition of this historic domain, when in 1854 came
to its occupancy, the vanguard of the colony of farmers from New
Jersey, Pennsylvania, New York, the New England States, and States
of the West, who bought large areas of the worn-down but desirable
lands, and commenced that work of restoration and improvement
which has been attended with such remarkable success.

At that time there were but three white families on the whole estate.
Now they number nearly forty families, and cultivate farms varying
in extent from twenty-five to three hundred acres, with values of from
fifty to five hundred dollars per acre.

In the year 1856 was incorporated by the Legislature of Virginia
the "Mount Vernon Ladies' Association of the Union," having for
its object the restoration of the "mansion and grounds," and the
reverential care thenceforth of everything pertaining to them. With
this idea in view, donations were solicited from the patriotic women
of the republic, and the "Home and Tomb" with two hundred acres
of the surrounding lands were purchased of John Augustine Washington, for the sum of two hundred thousand dollars. The work of ob-
taining the necessary funds for this laudable purpose was begun in
great earnestness. Miss Pamela Cunningham, of South Carolina, all
honor to her name and services, and who by common consent had
taken charge of the work, was constituted first regent, or manager of
the association, and she appointed vice-regents in every State of the
Union as her assistants. Edward Everett now gave his tongue and
pen to the work. He went from city to city, like Peter the Hermit
pleading for the rescue of the Holy Sepulchre, delivering an oration
on the character of Washington for the fund. Within two years from
the first delivery of the oration, he paid into the treasury of the association fifty thousand dollars, an amount increased later to sixty-
eight thousand dollars. The vice-regents each appointed State com-
mittees, and the money raised was nearly all in dollar subscriptions.
In July, 1859, three years after the movement was inaugurated, and
one year before all the purchase-money was paid and a deed given,
the late proprietor allowed the work of restoration to begin,—the
work which has resulted in the admirable condition and arrangements
everywhere apparent. And may we not indulge the hope that hence-
forth this place, to which every patriotic American turns with pride
and reverence, may be safe from a relapse to the desolation from
which it was retrieved?

Your most humble Serv.t
Law.r Washington
Nov: 7.th 1745

LAWRENCE WASHINGTON, THE FOUNDER OF THE MOUNT VERNON HOME.

L AWRENCE WASHINGTON deserves more than the incidental notices which have been accorded to him in other chapters of this Hand-book. In our regard for the merits and career of his distinguished brother, on whom too much praise cannot be bestowed, we are apt to lose sight of the noble and magnanimous spirit which was so instrumental in moulding and shaping that character which shines with such transcendent lustre in the galaxy of our Revolutionary heroes. Fifteen years older than his brother George, he at once in his orphanage filled the place of the correct fraternal exemplar and paternal adviser. When Lawrence came up from the lower Potomac to the occupancy of the domain of twenty-five hundred acres "lying along and south of Little Hunting Creek," George accompanied him, and remained with him in the new house which he there builded in 1743, and named in honor of his old commander, Mount Vernon, until Thomas, Lord Fairfax, needed him to take up his compass and chain and establish the "huts and bounds" of his possessions in the valley of the Shenandoah.

Major Lawrence Washington was the second child and only surviving son of Augustine Washington, and was born in Westmoreland County, Virginia, in 1718. He was a man of correct habits and good business qualifications, and had mingled much with prominent personages of his time. He and his brother Augustine were among the organizers of the "Ohio Company" to explore the western country, encourage settlements, and conduct trade with the Indians. It was in his relations with this company that he won an enviable distinction, as did his brother George after him, by avowing himself an advocate of religious toleration at a time when the statutes of Virginia recognized but one religious faith. Never very strong physically, with the continued and increasing pressure of his public duties in the state council and the land company, his health gave way, and in 1751, accompanied by his brother George, he went for healing to the Island of Barbadoes, but receiving no relief he returned to die at his Mount Vernon home, July, 1752. His marriage with Annie Fairfax had been blessed by four children, three of whom had died. His surviving child, Sarah, was still an infant at the time of her father's death. After providing in his will for his wife, he left Mount Vernon to his daughter, but in the event of her death without heirs, it was to go to his "beloved brother George." This daughter died within a year, and George inherited the "Home" before he was twenty-one years of age.

BELVOIR—THE OLD COLONIAL SEAT OF THE VIRGINIA FAIRFAXES.

They come, the shapes of joy and woe;
The airy crowds of long ago;
The dreams and fancies known of yore,
That have been but shall be no more:
They change the cloisters of the night
Into a garden of delight;
They make the dark and dreary hours
Open and blossom into flowers.

A SHORT distance below the mansion of Mount Vernon, just across the beautiful Bay of Dogue Creek, was situated a manorial estate, densely wooded, and many hundreds of acres in extent. It was a part of a very extensive domain known as the northern neck of Virginia, comprising in its area the twenty-three counties embraced between the head-waters of the Potomac and Rappahannock Rivers, and exceeding in extent more than five millions of acres. This region of country had been granted by letters-patent in 1688 from James the Second of England to Lord Thomas Culpeper, once Governor of Virginia from 1682 to 1686. From him it had descended through his daughter, Catharine Culpeper Fairfax, to her son Thomas, sixth Lord Fairfax of his line, a man of learning, a graduate of Oxford College and member of a literary club, of which the celebrated Addison was the leading spirit, and to whose pens we are indebted for the "Spectator." He was a grandson of Thomas Fairfax, the renowned general of the parliamentary or roundhead armies of Oliver Cromwell. By the terms of the original patent to Culpeper, he was constituted sole proprietor of the soil of this wilderness empire, with authority to divide, sell, grant, and occupy at his will, always, however, to be under allegiance to the royal prerogative, as was the common phraseology of grants in the days of feudalism. A royal gift, indeed, was this grant to one royal subject.

To the fine estate on the Potomac, first mentioned in the year 1738, came Colonel William Fairfax, a cousin of Lord Thomas, from Yorkshire, England, and founded the home which he named "Belvoir," for Belvoir Castle was one of the most celebrated of the English castles, and one of the finest of the present day. The manorial residence which he built, one of ample dimensions and appointments for the time, had a situation which commanded extended and charming views of the river and its environs. Washington, in his diary, incidentally tells us that it was "built of bricks and of ample dimensions, of two stories, with wide passages and cellars, and convenient offices, hall for servants, stables and coach-house, and with a large garden adjacent, stored with a great variety of fruits, all in good condition." The writer visited the ruins, early in the spring of the present year and traced out, and measured the foundations, and found them to be of the following dimensions: the foundations of the main building, sixty by thirty-six feet, with walls twenty-seven inches thick and cemented by mortar made from oyster shells, which had become extremely hard and tenacious. The cellar had occupied the whole area, and was seven

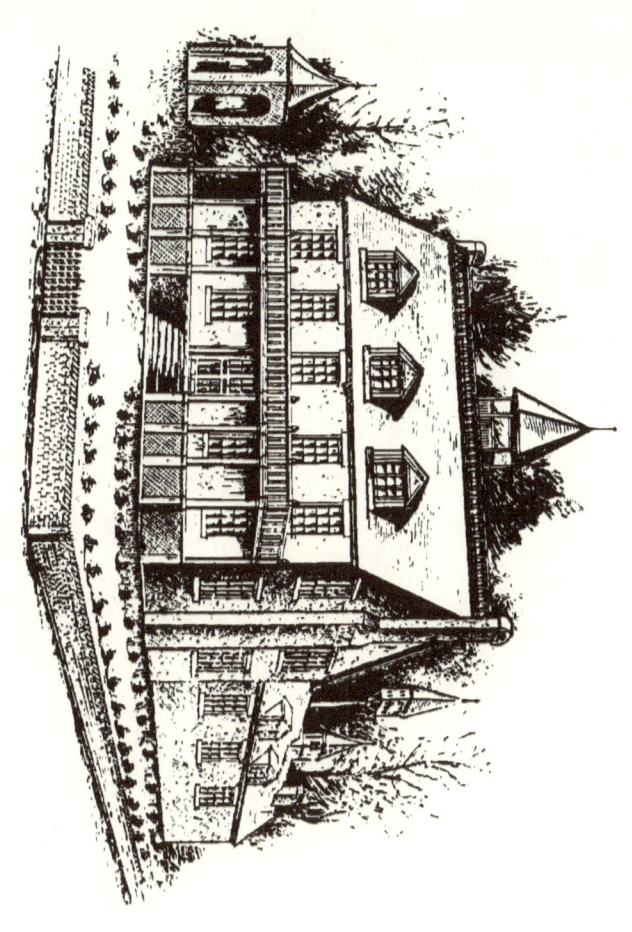

AN IDEAL OF "OLD BELVOIR MANSION."

RUINS OF BELVOIR MANSION.

feet deep, with partition walls twenty-four inches in thickness, with pavements of bricks seven inches square and four inches thick. Outside of the gable walls were heaps of quarry stones, denoting that there had been outside chimneys with large foundations. Everything about the parts of the walls still left intact, told of massiveness. Large trees had grown up from the *débris* inside of the foundations, and briars everywhere trailing gave to the spot a desolate appearance. The mansion had been enclosed by a wall of bricks, the wide foundations of which may still be traced through their entire extent of one hundred and fifty by one hundred feet. Adjacent are the ruins of five other brick buildings, presumably the great kitchen, the coacherie, and quarters for the house-servants; and in front, on the river bank, two hundred feet above the rippling tide, were the ruins of the summer house, which had commanded so many pleasant views and fair prospects. There is but an acre or so of cleared ground about the ruins. This must have been the site of the "garden," for there were thousands of daffodils waving their golden petals in the morning breeze, just as they had done when my Lady Fairfax was wont to tread those now neglected paths in the long, long years before. Through all the time of the coming and going of the many spring times, they had faithfully kept up their bright successions, and were yet remaining, silent mementos of the kindly care of vanished hands. But every vestige of the choice fruit trees described by Washington had disappeared, saving some veteran pear and cherry trees, which were yet thrifty-looking and white with bloom. A grape-vine eight inches in diameter was still vigorous by the fallen walls, its branches again putting forth buds with the return of another spring. The wells, from out of whose cooling depths so many refreshing draughts had been drawn by the "old oaken bucket" for man and beast, were choked and dry. The desolation was complete. But the morning sun was shining warm and radiant over it all. The buds of the forest boughs were opening into foliage. The glad spring birds were lightly flitting, and chirping their songs of love ; and hard by, the rippling waters of the beautiful river, were hurrying on in their seaward course, just as when the watchful eyes and careful hands of the masters were there, to order and direct all things aright.

In the wood near adjoining, rows of sunken mounds indicated the family burial-place. A score of graves may still be counted, without stone or vestige of enclosure. The marble slabs which had marked the last resting-places of William Fairfax and Deborah, his wife, the first master and mistress, and which had remained intact until a few years before the war, had been sacrilegiously broken up and carried away. Surely, this place of sepulture, so neglected and forlorn, ought to be enclosed, and receive from some friendly hands that care and attention which the eminent worth, of at least one of those whose ashes are there entombed, so well deserves. The old road may still be traced, from the mansion down to the river's edge, over which Washington so often passed, in his visits by water to his friends the Fairfaxes.

Here at Belvoir, in those primitive times, lived like feudal magnates, the representatives of the honorable Fairfax family, who, marrying and giving in marriage with other noted scions of Virginia, saw their wealth and influence steadily increase, as the years passed on.

As we behold the mansion now, in imagination, after the lapse of a century and a half, with the help of, not only Washington's description, but with that of accounts gathered from old inhabitants of the neighborhood many years since dust, and with the aid of the tracings of the ruins already described, our idea is that of a stately manor house, very similar, in outline and finish, to most of the old colonial dwellings still to be seen in Virginia, down to two generations ago. It has two stories and an attic, with steep over-jutting roofs, dormer windows, and huge outside chimneys of stone. There are belfry, and outlook, and ample verandas, for the summer breezes and views of the near flowing river. Within, the halls and rooms are spacious, with high ceilings, wainscoted and panelled walls, and the fireplaces are wide for warmth and cheery flames. This is our ideal of the "Belvoir House." There is not only a "fruit garden as has been stated," with bountiful supply of varieties of fruits, but there is a garden of flowers where "my lady Fairfax" has her box-bordered beds of lady's-slippers, sweet-williams, marigold shrubs, lilacs, and the like; and there are winding paths, and carriage-ways around the mansion, which lead down under the branches of great oaks, to the edge of the rippling waters or out into the broad fields.

The apartments of the Belvoir House, judging from a partial inventory of the household effects sold at the two public sales in 1774, must have been furnished as luxuriously as any old England manor house of the time. The purchases made by Washington alone, amounted to nearly two hundred pounds sterling.

William Fairfax, the first proprietor, was born in 1691, and was the grandson of Henry Fairfax, second son of fourth Lord Fairfax and Anna Harrison Fairfax. He had received a collegiate education, had seen much of the world, and his mind had been enriched and ripened by varied and venturous experience. Of an ancient English family, he had entered the army at the age of twenty-one, and subsequently had served with honor in the royal navy, both in the East and the West Indies,—had officiated as governor of New Providence, after having aided in rescuing the town from pirates, also, had fought valiantly for his sovereign, Queen Anne, in Spain, under Colonel Martin Bladen; and after coming to Belvoir, we find him a member of his majestie's honorable council of Virginia, and at one time, its presiding officer. Having married in the Bahamas, Sarah, daughter of Major Walker of Nassau, she accompanied him to England. Previous to his coming to Belvoir, he filled an appointment, from 1725 to 1734, as collector of customs in New Salem, in the province of Massachusetts. There, his first wife died, and was buried. His son George William was born in Nassau. Three of his children were born in Salem. Thomas, of the royal navy, was killed in battle, Annie married Lawrence Washington, and was the first mistress of Mount Vernon; and Sarah married John Carlyle of Alexandria, Virginia, who was a major and commissary, in the French and Indian War. By a second marriage, with Deborah Clark of Salem, he had three children,—Brian,

GRAVES OF WILLIAM AND DEBORAH FAIRFAX.

" Where shall once the wanderer weary
    Meet his resting place and shrine;
Under palm trees by the Ganges,
    Under lindens of the Rhine?

Shall I somewhere in the desert
    Owe my grave to stranger hands?
Or upon some lonely seashore
    Rest at last beneath the sands?

'Tis no matter! God's wide heaven
    Must surround me there as here;
And as death-lamps o'er me swinging
    Night by night the stars burn clear."

eighth Lord Fairfax, born in 1732 and died in 1802 ; William Henry, killed at the storming of Quebec in 1759 ; and Hannah, who married Warner Washington, cousin to George Washington.

William Fairfax had come to Virginia to act as agent for his cousin, Lord Thomas, in the management of his estates ; and in 1739 came also for the first time the Lord Proprietor himself, to become better acquainted with his wilderness possessions. After a year's sojourn he returned to England, but as he had been so well pleased by the Virginia country, its climate, and resources, after settling up his affairs there, and giving to his cousin Robert, his Kentish estates, also selling out his army commission, he came back in 1746, and for six years made his home at Belvoir, preparatory to his future and last home beyond the Blue Ridge in the Shenandoah Valley.

William Fairfax, we are informed by a contemporary writer, lived at his Belvoir home in the style of an English gentleman, surrounded by an intelligent and cultivated family of sons and daughters. He died in 1757. His wife Deborah ~~survived him but a few years~~. *died 1747* The ashes of both are in the neglected family burying-ground at Belvoir.

A marble tablet, bearing the following inscription, was still intact over the grave of Deborah until within a few years before the war, but not a vestige of it now remains.

Here rest the remains of Deborah Clark Fairfax, who departed this troublesome life on the fourteenth day of ~~——~~, 1759, in the ~~thirty~~ *sixty* seventh year of her age. She was the ~~daughter~~ of Francis Clark, of New Salem, Massachusetts colony, and late wife of William Fairfax, Esqr., collector of his Majestie's customs on south Potomac, and one of the King's honorable council of Virginia. In every station of life worthy of imitation. A faithful and loving wife. The best of mothers. A sincere and amiable friend. In all religious duties well instructed and observant, and has gone where only such virtues can be rewarded.

George William Fairfax, born 1724, succeeded to his father's estate. He had been educated in England, as was then the custom generally, with the sons of the wealthy colonists, after which he resided for some time at Belvoir. His wife was Sarah, daughter of Colonel William Cary, of Hampton, Virginia. In 1747 he accompanied Washington over the mountains, and assisted him in his three years' survey of the lands of the Proprietor in the Shenandoah Valley. In 1773, accompanied by his wife, he went to England to look after some property he had inherited there. On his way over he passed the ships which brought to the colonies the ill-fated cargoes of tea, which were either burned or thrown overboard into the harbors of Boston and Annapolis. Washington consented to act as his agent in his absence, supposing that it would be of but short duration. But owing to long delays in the settlement of his business affairs, he never returned to his Virginia home. He finally directed his agent to sell his household furniture and the stock on the plantation, and lease the premises of Belvoir. A sale was accordingly held on the estate in

1774, which continued two days, and a further sale was held in December of the same year. The property was then leased for seven years to Rev. Andrew Martin, but in a short time after, the mansion was destroyed by fire. The owner's long absence, and the fact that the old home was desolate, together with the excitement and derangement of business incident to the war for independence, caused the estate to rapidly depreciate. Early in 1775 Washington relinquished the agency of the George William Fairfax business, as his time was fully taken up in directing the momentous affairs of the Revolution.

The proprietors of Mount Vernon and Belvoir and their families were always on the most friendly terms, as the letters extant of each attest. Mr. Fairfax favored the early protests against the unjust acts of Great Britain and the petitions to the king in the interests of the colonies, but opposed measures looking to forcible resistance.

He was for many years a member of the House of Burgesses, and it was on his account that during the election of 1754, when he was opposed by Colonel Elzy, that his friend General Washington engaged in the acrimonious controversy with Mr. Payne in the market-place of Alexandria.

During the war which ensued, some of the property of George Fairfax in Fairfax County was escheated to the State. His loss of income from America forced him to limit his expenses. He therefore removed from Yorkshire to Bath and lived in a modest way, dividing generously his limited means with American prisoners held in England. He left Belvoir and some other landed property to Ferdinando, third son of his half-brother, Rev. Bryan Fairfax, and died at Bath, England, April 3, 1787, and was buried in Wirthlington Church. His will appointed George Washington as one of his executors. His wife survived him until 1812. Bryan Fairfax, third son of William Fairfax, married a daughter of Wilson Cary, and his residence in Fairfax County was known as Towlston Hall, near Hunting Creek Bridge. He was a brother-in-law of Lawrence Washington, a friend of George Washington, and at one time was chaplain in the army by his appointment. Ferdinando, eighth lord, died at Mount Eagle, near Alexandria, in 1820, at the age of forty-six. Bryan Fairfax was rector of Christ Church from 1790 to 1792, and went to England in 1793 to claim the peerage after the death of Robert, the seventh lord, who never lived in this country. The title was confirmed to him in 1800. During the last years of his life he was a Swedenborgian. Here is his epitaph—

IN MEMORIAM.

RIGHT HON. AND REV. BRYAN
LORD FAIRFAX,
BARON OF CAMERON, RECTOR OF
FAIRFAX PARISH,
DIED AT M^T EAGLE, AUG. 7,
1802, AGED 75.

Years ago this fine estate of Belvoir with its two thousand acres of good farming lands passed from the hands of the Fairfax family; and with the exception of about two hundred and fifty acres the entire area has lapsed back to a veritable wilderness, chiefly of pines and cedars, which have grown up from the ridges still everywhere to be seen of the old corn and tobacco crops. Once nearly every acre of its arable portions was under tillage, but as the impoverishing process of cropping without renumeration to the soil went on through the generations as was so often the case in old Virginia, the worn-out acres here and there were abandoned to the invasion of the wiry sedge grass and wild wood growth. The encroachments were slow but sure, for there were no hands to check or stay its progress. Now, this wilderness is awaiting the coming of axes and hoes and ploughs which, in the hands of capable, industrious, and practical settlers, will reverse the order of nature, clear the cumbered lands, turn anew the kindly furrows, scatter again the seeds, gather again the harvests, and build up in the wastes, homes of comfort, with gardens and orchards, and all the surroundings which make rural life so pleasant and desirable. Almost within sight of the National Capital, lying on tide water, and near to the line of the new Electric Railway, the realization of all these possibilities cannot, we think, be so very remote; and some lover of the picturesque and beautiful, with historic pride and veneration for the associations of the "dear, dead past beyond recall," which linger all around the famous locality by the " grand old river," will we trust come with ample means and classic taste, and on the foundations of the old Fairfax home erect a structure which will be worthy of the superb situation and the story of its memorable events.

The curious wayfarer of our time who strays by the site of the once stately mansion of Belvoir will find only fallen walls, blackened hearthstones, mounds of briar-grown bricks and rubbish to mark the historic spots where through so many years went on the long forgotten routine of domestic events and incidents of colonial life in the Fairfax family successions. Of all these events and incidents which would be fraught with so much interest to the present generation, only the most fragmentary accounts have come down to us through either written record or word of tradition. Only here and there a canvas memory—some familiar names, and some wandering, vague report of grace and loveliness and gallant exploit. Their failings are lost sight of and no longer dwell in living recollection. Let them so remain, bright images gilded by the sunlight of the past and clad in all their halo of romance—with nothing hidden by the distance but their human imperfections. We know that in connection with Mount Vernon this home of the Fairfaxes was one of the chief social centres of the tide-water region of the Old Dominion, with always open doors and a generous hospitality for the coming guest. We know that within its walls our Washington was an ofttimes and welcome guest. From Mount Vernon it was but a few minutes' sail or pull with the oars ; and well he knew how to handle both. Here it was that he met the charming Miss Mary Cary, sister of Mrs. George Fairfax, and became conscious for the first time in his stripling years of the conquering fascinations of female charms, only to be denied afterwards the coveted privilege of being a suitor and claimant of the hand and heart of the young lady by the stern and unyielding father, who failed to perceive in the young aspirant a prospect of that wealthy and influential alliance which he had contemplated for his daughter. "His heiress," said the haughty old cavalier, "had been used to riding in her own chariot attended by servitors." The love-lorn youth pressed no more his claim after such an unexpected rebuff, and never saw her but once again. That was when he nodded to her pallid and fainting visage in a window of the old capital of Williamsburg, when he rode through on his triumphal march with waving banners and music playing from the surrender of Cornwallis at Yorktown. We know also that Lord Thomas Fairfax, the proprietor, the scholar and graduate of Oxford, and the friend of Addison, the whilom devotee of fashion and gayety in old London town, and the jilted and inconsolable lover, was for years a dweller under the same hospitable roof. We know, too, that in those halls were gravely talked over and considered by many great minds of the time various measures for the public weal in the infant colony preparatory to their proposal and final enactment in the House of Burgesses at the vice-regal capital of Williamsburg. This is all of the story which has come down to us through the long lapse of the years. The rest of it for the most part is silent forever with the dust of the many actors of those times. Some of it may still be preserved in musty letters and other papers of old lofts and garrets, some time it may be to be rescued and unfolded for the curious listener by faithful chroniclers yet to come. But in our fondness for all such reminiscences of the olden times, we may go back in imagination through the dim and shadowy vistas of the past, and giving loose rein to fancy, let it summon up and reincarnate for us the many other honored guests of high degree who came and went from year to year over those thresholds as social or other occasions invited.

Let us for a time be spectators within those old halls with their massive oaken doors and wide fireplaces, and their wainscoted and panelled walls, whereon hang fowling-pieces and antlers of the chase, and from which look down ancestral faces, and appear pictures of old castles and scenes of battle. Many shadowy forms stand out in strange outline before our wondering visions. We smile at their quaint costumes and their ways of speech, but they are men and women well bred, with courtly manners and comely lineaments, and they please us well by their easy dignity and stately demeanor. They pass on and vanish. Another group comes up—a group of neighbors and friends listening intently to the "freshest advices" by the latest ship just in from London, Amsterdam, or Barbadoes to Alexandria or Dumfries, it may have been, after a voyage of weeks or months. The London *Gazette* informs them of the "wars and rumors of wars" in Europe, of the campaigns in Germany and India, and of the course of hostilities between England and France; and precious letters are read telling of how all is going with friends they left behind them in the homes so far away over the seas.

OLD HOUSE ON THE BELKNAP ESTATE

The scene changes. Strains of music are floating on the air, and ladies fair and gay gallants bow gracefully to each other and trip gayly through the mazes of the minuet. Meanwhile, as the music and the dance go on, my Lord Thomas sits complacently in his easy arm-chair, attired in velvet coat, and ruff, doublet and silken hose and buckles. His dancing days are over, for he has passed his three-score milestone, and his hair is well silvered o'er, but he watches as intently the gliding figures over the oaken floor, and, mayhap, his thoughts are far away in halls of Yorkshire or Kent, or old London, when in his heyday of life he, too, had tripped as gayly with the giddy girl who had so cruelly won his heart and then played him false for another. The old baron is genial and kindly to all, and everybody is fond of him and graciously defers to his lineage and experience. He chats pleasantly with the guests, delights in their merriment, and, anon, in drowsy mood, goes nodding, and then passes away to the land of dreams. We linger still, and the scene again changes. The blessed Christmas tide comes round. The busy note of preparation is rife in parlor and kitchen. The hickory yule logs are piled and lighted, and their cheery and warming flames go trooping up the great stone chimneys into the midwinter night. The holly branches and mistletoe boughs are hung on the walls. Genial and convivial friends, young and old, come in from anear and afar, and there is full measure of kindly feeling and good cheer and a jocund time for all. The bounti-ful board smokes as in old England's manorial homesteads with savory venison, wild turkey, and the wild boar's head from the surrounding forests. As we wait still longer in the shadows of the old mansion we may give still wider range to fancy, and call up to view scenes of mirth and rejoicing, as when joyous bridal bells were chiming; or scenes of sorrow and mourning, as when funeral bells were tolling. And, waiting still longer with the coming and going of the years, we may note the passing out over the threshold of the old mansion its master and mistress, to take that long voyage across the ocean which was to separate them forever from their Virginia home. And yet a little longer we will wait, till the household heirlooms and treasures are sold under the hammer of the auctioneer and are scattered widely over the land, and finally, till that baleful day comes, when those storied walls go down in fire and crumble to dust, and there is an end to all the times of glad meetings and good cheer—of all the times of song and music and the dance and of all the kindly greetings and farewells at the ancient homestead of Belvoir.

> The years
> Have gone, and with them many a glorious throng
> Of happy dreams. Their mark is on each brow,
> Their shadows in each heart. In their swift course
> They waved their sceptres o'er the beautiful,
> And they are not. They laid their pallid hands
> Upon the strong man, and the haughty form
> Is fallen, and the flashing eye is dim—
> They trod the hall of revelry, where throng'd
> The bright and joyous, and the tearful wail
> Of stricken ones is heard where erst the song
> And reckless shout resounded.

These are only the picturings of fancy, and to many they may seem idle and vague, even foolish; but they are picturings which some of us love to linger over, and are loth to let pass from our visions, for they touch responsive chords of our hearts and set them to rhythm and accord with all that belongs to those remote but cherished times; and as the vistas lengthen and grow dimmer we shall but cling to them and love them all the more.

Scattered over the tide-water region of Virginia are hundreds of such heaps of bricks and stones as those to be seen on the site of the old house of Belvoir we have been describing; and they arrest the attention of the thoughtful passer and tell to him mute but pathetic and impressive stories of the past, of rural mansions of the great Virginia estates where culture, refinement, and a generous hospitality abounded. Only a few of the typical old buildings remain for us, and these are passing rapidly from view, and the time is not far distant when the last of these landmarks of the vice-regal and revolutionary times will be no more.

GREENWAY COURT.

NOT far from the little village of Millwood, in the Shenandoah Valley, there stood a few years ago an ancient mansion of peculiar interest. It was plainly a relic of the remote past—quaint in style, and suggestive to the beholder of strange circumstances and histories. Tall locusts of a century's growth surrounded it, and waved their spreading branches over its steep roofs and windows.

This ancient mansion was once the home of an English nobleman, who only chanced to live in Virginia, and did not directly influence in any considerable measure the events of the period in which he was an actor. And what, it may be asked, had Thomas, Lord Fairfax, Baron of Cameron, the sixth of the name, of Greenway Court in the Shenandoah Valley, to do with the history of his era? What did he perform? and why is a place demanded for him in our annals? The answer is not difficult. With this notable person who has passed to his long rest, and lies nearly forgotten in the old church at Winchester, is connected a name which will never be forgotten. His was the high mission to shape in no small measure the immense strength of George Washington. His hand pointed attention to the rising planet of this great life, and opened its career toward the zenith—the planet which shines now the polar star of our liberties, set in the stormy skies of the Revolution. The brilliance of that star no man can now increase nor obscure, as no cloud can dim it,—and yet, once it was unknown, and needed assistance, which Lord Fairfax afforded.

Any account of the youth of Washington must involve no small reference to the old fox-hunting Baron who took an especial fancy for him when he was a boy of sixteen, and greatly aided in developing his capabilities and character. Fairfax not only thus shaped by his counsels the unfolding mind of the young man, but placed the future leader of the American Revolution in that course of training which hardened his muscles, toughened his manhood, taught him self-reliance, and gave him that military repute in the public eye, which secured

GREENWAY COURT.

for him at a comparatively early age the appointment of commander-
in-chief of the Continental armies over all competitors. First and
last, Fairfax was the fast and continuing friend of Washington, and
not even the struggle for independence, in which they espoused opposite sides, operated to weaken this regard. In imagination let us
look at this old house in which Lord Thomas passed about thirty years
of his bachelor life. It stands before us on a green knoll,—solitary,
almost, in the great wilderness, and all its surroundings impress us
with ideas of pioneer life and habits. It is a long, low building, constructed of the limestone of the region. A row of dormer windows
stands prominently out from its steep over-hanging roof, and massive
chimneys of stone appear outside of its gables which are studded
with coops around which swarm swallows and martins. From the
ridge of the roof rise two belfries or lookouts, constructed probably
by the original owner to give the alarm in case of an invasion by the
savages. Not many paces from the old mansion was a small log house
in which the eccentric proprietor slept, surrounded by his dogs, of
which he was passionately fond ; the large edifice having been assigned
to his steward. A small cabin of stone near the north end of the house
was his office ; and in this he transacted all the business of his vast
possessions, giving quit-rents, signing deeds, and holding audiences to
adjust claims and boundary lines. Scattered over the knoll were the
quarters for his many servants. And here in the midst of dogs and
horses, backwoodsmen, Indians, half-breeds, and squatters, who feasted
daily at his plentiful board, the fine gentleman of Pall Mall, the friend
of Joseph Addison, passed more than a quarter of a century. He lived
in this frontier locality the life of a recluse. He had brought with him
an ample library of books, and these were welcome companionship for
him in his solitary hours. Ten thousand acres of land around his un-
pretentious lodge he had allotted for a manorial estate, with the design
at some time of erecting upon it a castle for a residence ; this design
he never executed.

At the age of twenty-five, Lord Fairfax was one of the gayest of the
young men of London society. He went the rounds of dissipation
with the fondest enjoyment, and was considered one of the finest
beaux of his day. He was well received by all classes. Young noblemen, dissipating rapidly their patrimonial substance, found in him a
congenial companion in their intrigues and revels. Countesses permitted him to kiss their jewelled hands; and when he made his bow
in their drawing-rooms, received him with their most patronizing
smiles. But our young lord after a time found himself arrested in his
gay round of pleasures in the haunts of silk stockings and hooped
petticoats. He had revolved like a gayly-colored moth about many
beautiful luminaries without singeing his wings. But his hour of fate
came. One of the beauties of the time transfixed him. He circled
in closer and closer gyrations. His pinions were caught in the blaze,
and he was a hopeless captive. My Lord Fairfax no longer engaged
in revels or the rounds of dissipation, but like a sensible lover ac-
cepted the new conditions, and sought only to make everything ready
for a life of real happiness in the nuptials of two loving and con-

fiding hearts. He turned resolutely from the frivolous past and looked only to the promising future, which he saw as if unfolding something higher and more substantial for his achievement and enjoyment, and then the real sweetness and depth of his truer nature revealed themselves from beneath the wrappings of dissipation and vice. He gave up everything which had pleased him for this woman; and all that he now asked was permission to take his affianced away from the dangerous atmosphere of the court, and to live with her peacefully as a good nobleman of the provinces. He loved her passionately, and wished to discard all who threatened to interfere with the exclusive enjoyment of her society. All his resources were taxed to supply the most splendid marriage gifts; and absorbed in this delightful dream of love, his happiness was raised to the empyrean. But he was destined to have a sudden awakening from his dream, a terrible, almost fatal fall from his cloudland. He had expended the wealth of his deep and earnest nature on a coquette,—his goddess was a woman simply,—and a very shallow one. She threw Fairfax carelessly overboard, and married a nobleman who won her by the superior attractions of a ducal coronet. Thus struck doubly in his pride and his love, Fairfax looked around him in despair for some retreat to which he might fly and forget in a measure his sorrows. London was hateful to him, the country no less distasteful. He could not again plunge into the mad whirl of the one, nor rust away in the dull routine of the other. His griefs demanded action to dissipate them,—adventure, new scenes, another land were needed. This process of reflection turned the young man's thoughts to the lands in far away Virginia which he held in right of his mother, the daughter of Lord Culpeper, to whom they had originally been granted; and finally he bade adieu to England and came over the seas. Such were the events in the early life of this gentleman which brought him to Virginia.

The house of Belvoir to which Lord Fairfax came was the residence, as has already been stated, of Sir William Fairfax, his cousin, to whom he had entrusted the management of his Virginia lands. Lawrence Washington, the eldest brother of George, had married a daughter of Sir William; and here commences the connection of the already aged proprietor and the boy of sixteen who was to lead the armies of the Revolution. Washington was a frequent inmate of the Belvoir home; and the boy was the chosen companion of the old lord in his hunting expeditions. In the reckless sports of the field the proprietor seemed to find the chief solace for his love-lorn griefs. Time slowly dissipated his despairing recollections, however, and now, as he approached the middle of that century the dawn of which had witnessed so much of his misery, the softer traits of his character returned, and he was to those for whom he felt regard a most delightful and instructive companion. Almost every trace of personal attraction, though, had left him. Upwards of six feet in stature, gaunt, raw-boned, near-sighted, with light gray eyes, and a sharp aquiline nose, he was scarcely recognizable as the elegant young nobleman of the days of Queen Anne. But time and reflection had mellowed his mind, and when he pleased, the old gentleman could enchain his hearers with brilliant conversation of which his early training and experiences had given him very great command. He had seen all the great characters of the period of his youth, had watched the unfolding of events, and studied their causes. All the social history, the scandalous chronicles, the private details of celebrated personages had been familiar to him ; and his conversation thus presented a glowing picture of the past. Something of cynical wit still clung to him, and the fireside of Belvoir was the scene of much satiric comments between the old nobleman and his cousin William. But Fairfax preserved great fondness for youth, and took especial pleasure in the society of our George of Mount Vernon. He not only took him as a companion in his hunts, but liked to have the boy with him when he walked out ; and it may be easily understood that the talks of the exile had a deep effect upon young Washington.

The import of Lord Fairfax's connection with the future commander-in-chief lies chiefly in the commission which he intrusted to the boy of seventeen, that of surveying and laying out his vast possession in the Shenandoah Valley. Providence here as everywhere seemed to have directed the movements of man to work out its own special ends. This employment as surveyor on the wilderness frontiers was the turning-point in the young man's life, and the results of the expedition of three years in its influences on his habits and character, the information and self-reliance it gave him, and the hardships it taught him to endure are now the property of history.

It is not a part of our design to follow the young surveyor in his expedition which led him from Greenway Court to the headwaters of the Potomac where Cumberland now stands, and thence into the wilderness of the "Great South Branch," a country as wholly unknown as it was fertile and magnificent. He returned to Mount Vernon a new being, and the broad foundation of his character was laid.

The first act of his eventful life had been played—the early lessons of training and endurance thoroughly learned—the scene of his subsequent exertions fixed ; and the prudence, courage, coolness, and determination which he displayed on this arena, made him general in chief when the crisis came, of the forces of the Revolutionary struggle. Lord Fairfax had given him the impetus. From him he received the direction of his genius, and to the attentive student of these early events the conviction becomes more and more absolute that Lord Fairfax was the great "influence" of his life. And the interest attaching to the career of this noble patron consists chiefly in his connection with the life of the rising hero. Having formed as we have seen in no small measure the character of the boy of seventeen he lived to receive the tidings that this boy had overthrown forever the dominion of Great Britain in America on the field of Yorktown. So had Providence decreed ; and the gray-haired baron doubtless felt that he was only the humble instrument in that all powerful Hand.

After Yorktown—after the supreme defeat of the proud English general by the lad whom he had trained, it was "time for him to die." His death took place in 1781, at the age of ninety-three, and his body lies buried in the old Episcopal churchyard at Winchester, Va. His barony and its prerogatives according to English law descended in the absence of a son to his eldest brother Robert, who thus became seventh Lord Fairfax. The latter died in Leed's Castle, England, 1791, without a son. The baronial title then fell to Rev. Bryan Fairfax, son of William and brother-in-law of Lawrence Washington. His place was Towlston Hall, Mount Eagle, on Hunting Creek, Fairfax County, Va. He died in 1802.

The estate of Greenway Court of ten thousand acres descended to relatives of the proprietor in England. The lodge or mansion, like that of Belvoir on the Potomac, went down in fire.

WOOD LAWN MANSION, THE HOME OF NELLY CUSTIS.

ONE of the most beautiful young women of her time was Eleanor Parke Custis, a granddaughter of Martha Washington and an adopted daughter of General Washington. Her portrait, painted by Gilbert Stuart, was the most attractive picture among the rare paintings at Arlington House, the residence of her brother, George W. Parke Custis, for about fifty years. It is the likeness of a maiden when about eighteen years of age, the admired of all who attended the republican court during the last year of Washington's administration.

She is dressed in a plain white garment, in the scant fashion of the day, one of her plump, bare arms forming a conspicuous feature of the picture, her chin resting upon a finger of her gently closed hand. Her sweet face, regular in every feature, is garnished by her dark curls, tastefully clustering around her forehead and temples, while her long hair, gathered in an apparently careless manner on the top of her head, is secured by a cluster of white flowers. The whole picture is modest, simple, beautiful.

"Nelly Custis," as she was called in her maidenhood, was as witty as she was beautiful; quick at repartee, highly accomplished, full of information, a good conversationalist, the life of any company whether young or old and was greatly beloved by her foster-father, the great patriot. When in June, 1775, Washington was appointed Commander-in-Chief of the Continental Army, he placed John Parke Custis, the father of "Nelly," on his staff, in which capacity he served during most of the long war that followed. He was aide to Washington at the siege of Yorktown in the autumn of 1781, and was then a member of the Virginia Assembly, but dying that year of fever, his children, George W. Parke Custis and Eleanor Parke Custis, were left orphans, the former nearly three years old and the latter only six months old, and became the adopted children of Washington.

Washington had a favorite nephew, Lawrence, a son of his sister Betty Lewis. He was much at Mount Vernon after Washington's retirement from the presidency, and the "blessing" of a "good husband" for Nelly when she would "want and deserve one" was bestowed upon her. She and Lawrence Lewis were married February 22, 1799. Many suitors had sought her hand, to be denied for the one whom her

THE END OF GREENWAY COURT.

WOODLAWN MANSION.

Home of Nelly Custis

(Page 68)

grandfather had chosen and preferred for her over all others. About a month before the happy event the patriot wrote to his nephew, say-ing, "Your letter of January 10th,I received in Alexandria on Monday, whither I went to become the guardian of Nelly, thereby to authorize a license for your nuptials on the 22d of next month." The wedding took place on the last anniversary of his birthday that Washington spent on earth. Great preparations had been made for the event. The mansion was decked with flowers and evergreens, and ample provision made for a time of festivity and good cheer ; and the gentlefolk of the surrounding country invited. There were assembled for the occa-sion the Dandridges, Custises, Calverts, Lees, Lewises, Corbins, Bush-rods, Blackburns, Masons, Carrolls, and many others. The ceremony was performed in the great drawing-room lighted by many waxen tapers, which brought out in strong relief the silent portraits on the walls, in curious contrast with the merry throng below them. The stately minuet was danced and the spirited Virginia reel. Low voices whispered tender words in hall and anterooms, and the house soon to be so silent and mournful, echoed with mirth and hilarity. It was a brilliant scene. The picturesque costumes of the colonial days were still in vogue,—rich fabrics, and richer colors, stomachers, and short clothes. jewelled buckles and brooches, powder and ruffles every-where. Mount Vernon never witnessed such a scene again. Ten months later, in the same long drawing-room so lately the scene of these bridal festivities, the body of the great chief lay on its sable bier.

By a provision of the last will and testament of George Washing-ton, made July 9, 1799, "all that tract of land" in the county of Fairfax, and a portion of the Mount Vernon estate "north of the road leading from the ford of Dogue Run to the gum spring as de-scribed in the devise of the other part of the tract to Bushrod Wash-ington until it comes to the stone and three red or Spanish oaks on the knowl—thence with the rectangular line to the back line, between Mr. Mason and me—thence with that line westerly along the new double ditch to Dogue Run by the tumbling dam of my mill—thence with the said run to the ford aforementioned, to which I add all the land I possess west of said Dogue Creek, bounded easterly and south-erly thereby—together with the Mill and Distillery, and all other houses and improvements on the premises, making together about two thousand acres," was devised as a dower to the aforesaid Major Lewis and Nelly his wife. On this patrimonial estate these favored subjects of the general's solicitude erected in 1805 a commodious dwelling,— much more pretentious than that of Mount Vernon,—and began the establishment of their new home. Nelly was then just twenty-five years of age. It had been six years since she followed the remains of her honored grandfather to their last earthly resting-place, and Martha, her grandmother, had only three years before been laid by his side. They built their dwelling-place three miles inland from Mount Vernon, but on a high elevation, so that it commanded a pleasant view of the river and the expanse of Dogue Bay and its wide stretching valley.

Under the roof of Wood Lawn, as at Mount Vernon, was ever dis-

pensed a generous hospitality, and many were the distinguished visitors of the time from near and afar, who came to cross its threshold
and pay their regards to its well-beloved and accomplished matron.

Lafayette, on his second visit to the land he had so valiantly helped
to defend, came here in 1824 to renew his fondly-cherished acquaint-
ance with Nelly, the stately house-wife, who was but a child when he
had seen her before in the home of his old commander, and had taken
her in her laughing moods upon his knee and kissed her with a
parental fondness, remembering doubtless the dear ones of his own
household in *la belle* France. For nearly forty years Nelly was mistress of the Wood Lawn mansion, and here were born to her four children,—Agnes the eldest, dying at school in Philadelphia; Frances
Parke, who married General E. G. W. Butler, and died at Pass Christian, Mississippi, a few years ago; Lorenzo, and Eleanor Angela, who
married Hon. C. M. Conrad, of Louisiana, and died in New Orleans
many years ago. Major Lawrence Lewis died at Arlington, Novem-
ber 20, 1839, and one summer day, July 15, 1852, Mrs. Nelly, his wife,
followed him full of years and honors to the burial vault at Mount
Vernon. She had passed one year beyond the threescore and ten line.
To the watcher from farmhouse and village, that must have seemed a
lonely and mournful funeral procession, indeed, as it slowly wended
its course down the long Virginia highway from the Shenandoah to
the Potomac. The hearse containing the remains of the aged grandmother, and a solitary carriage accompanying, with the two surviving
grandsons, one of whom is still living to tell of the impressive circumstances of the event. Late at night their journey was finished,
and the coffined form of Nelly was placed in the parlor of Mount Vernon, where, more than fifty years before, crowned with bridal wreaths,
" the fairest lady of the land," Washington himself had affectionately
given her in marriage, and commended her to the love and protecting care of the one favored claimant of his choice, and where she
had received the congratulations and blessings of so many of her
kinsfolk and friends. Many of the citizens of Alexandria and Washington and the surrounding country came to pay their tributes of fond
remembrance and regard to " Nelly" as she lay in state in the
" mansion," and to see the last of " earth to earth." Down in the
family burial-place, just by the waters of the river on whose pleasant
banks she had passed so many happy days in childhood and youth, her
dust is very near to that of her kind and loving guardians. A
marble monument marks her last resting-place with the following inscription:

SACRED

to the memory of Eleanor Parke Custis, granddaughter of Mrs. Washington, and adopted daughter of General Washington. Reared under
the roof of the Father of his Country, this lady was not more remarkable for the beauty of her person than for the superiority of her mind.
She lived to be admired, and died to be regretted, July 15, 1852, in
the seventy-first year of her age.

On last Decoration Day the writer esteemed it a great pleasure to

strew her apparently neglected grave with flowers. Even in her last closing years, Nelly retained many traces of her early beauty and vivacity.

We have been told by her surviving grandson that the early home life and associations of Mount Vernon lingered ever with his grandmother as beatifying visions, and that she never wearied in recounting them to her children and grandchildren. A theme dearest of all to her heart was the story of her social relations with the fond and indulgent master and mistress of the Mount Vernon home whose passing away from her she long and deeply mourned.

"All who knew the subject of our sketch," says her aunt, Mrs. General Robert E. Lee, in her memoir of George W. Parke Custis, "were wont to recall the pleasure they had derived from her extensive information, brilliant wit, and boundless generosity. The most tender parent and devoted friend, she lived in the enjoyment of her affections. She was often urged to write her memoirs, which might even have surpassed in interest to her countrymen those of Madame de Sévigné and others of equal note, as her pen gave free expression to her lively imagination and clear memory. Would that we could recall the many tales of the past we have heard from her lips, but, alas! we should fail to give them accurately. One narrative is retained, as it made a strong impression at the time. She said the most perfect harmony always existed 'between her grandmamma and the general,' and that in all his intercourse with her he was most considerate and tender. She had often seen her when she had something to communicate, or a request to make of him at a moment when his mind was entirely abstracted from the present, seize him by the button to command his attention, when he would look down upon her with a benignant smile and become at once attentive to her wishes, which were never slighted. She also said that the grave dignity which he usually wore did not prevent his keen enjoyment of a joke, and that no one laughed more heartily than did he when she herself, a gay, laughing girl, gave one of her saucy descriptions of any scene in which she had taken part, or any one of the merry pranks she then often played; and that he would retire from the room in which her young companions were amusing themselves, because his presence caused a reserve which they could not overcome. But he always regretted it exceedingly, as their sports and enjoyments always seemed to interest him."

Of course, Washington was always Nelly's ideal hero, and the grandest of all the line of noble men.

General Zachary Taylor was one of her favorites among the public men of her time, and when he was elected to the presidency, she paid him a visit, and was for some time an honored guest in the White House, where she received the marked attentions of many distinguished personages of that day. While she lived she did not lose the hold she had in all her younger years upon the popular regard. She was still the storied, picturesque "Nelly" who had been the fondly petted child in the household of him who was "first in peace, first in war, and first in the hearts of his countrymen."

When that fair, smooth brow of the great artist's picture had been

imprinted with the lines of threescore years, and those clustering
curls had changed their brown to threads of snow, how she must have
seemed like some saintly messenger to those who eagerly listened to
her as she brought from memory's far-away shore the historic scenes
which had passed before those sparkling eyes in the heyday of her
youthful life. Lorenzo, her only son, inherited the Wood Lawn
estate, and resided for some years in the mansion. He was married
to Esther Maria Coxe, of Philadelphia, in 1827, and died in 1847.
His widow survived him until 1885. Of the six children of Lorenzo,
only one is left, J. R. C. Lewis, of Berryville, Clarke County, Virginia.
In 1845, the entire domain of this estate, having been almost entirely
neglected through many years, presented a most forlorn appearance.
Only here and there a patch of ground was under cultivation,—not a
handful of grass-seed was sown, not a ton of hay cut. The fields were
overgrown with sedge, brambles, sassafras, and cedars, and all traces of
fencing had disappeared. Not a white man was living on an acre of it.
Only a few superannuated slaves remained in some rickety cabins,
and these were subsisting on products from a farm in another county.
The tax assessment was thirty dollars –one cent and a half an acre,
although the buildings alone had cost near fifty thousand dollars, just
forty-three years before. It was at this period that the New Jersey
colony purchased the property for $12.50 per acre, and subsequently
the whole tract was divided and subdivided into small farms, and occupied by improving proprietors. The mansion, substantially constructed of old-fashioned bricks, having a main building sixty by
forty feet, with wide halls, spacious apartments, and ample wings
united by corridors to the main portion, together with sixty acres
of land, was recently purchased by the Electric Railway Company,
who propose in the near future to make it the lower terminus of their
road, in which event the "Old Mansion" will be faithfully restored
to its original beauty, and thenceforth be kept as an enduring memo-
rial of its first mistress, the beloved foster-daughter of George Washington. No more fitting place, we think, than this could be chosen
by the associations of the sons and daughters of the "Revolution"
for the holding of their annual reunions, and the keeping of their
archives and historic mementos and relics. That would make it a
desirable and attractive place of pilgrimage in all coming years, and
most effectually secure its perpetual preservation.

WASHINGTON'S MILL.

A T the head of Dogue Creek Bay are the ruins of the old stone
mill which in Washington's time ground all the grist of the
grain products of the Mount Vernon estate. The plash of the waters
over its wheel, and the clatter and din of its grinding gear have been
silent for threescore years. The raceway which led the waters from
the pond far up the valley across the fields to turn the wheel are now
grazing grounds for cattle ; but the shaky tenement stood until the
beginning of the fifties. The stones of the fallen walls have been

From
Your Grandmother,
E.P. Lewis.

Dec͟r 25͟th 1841.

(At three-score-and-ten.)

Mrs. Nelly Custis.

WASHINGTON'S OLD MILL.

At Epworanson, Head of Bogue Bay.

(Page 4.)

carted away and used in the foundations of houses in the neighborhood. All the meal for the plantation hands over the eight thousand acres was ground by this mill, and cargoes of flour were made by it and shipped to the West Indies and other places in schooners, which then came in the deeper waters, to load at its very doors. The picture as given is not an ideal of the old structure, but a truthful representation of it.

The locality of this old mill, once known as Epsecwasson, acquires additional interest from the very plausible supposition that here at the head of Dogue Bay, so named from an Indian tribe inhabiting its borders, was begun the first settlement and clearing of the "Hunting Creek" plantation of two thousand five hundred acres which about the year 1670 was assigned to John Washington, great-grandfather of the illustrious George Washington, as his share of a joint patent from Lord Culpeper.

This John Washington died in January, 1677. In his will he left this plantation to his son Lawrence, who had made some improvements on it, and at his death bequeathed it to his son Augustine, the father of the general. Augustine further improved and cultivated the plantation aforesaid, and in the division of his estate left it by will to his eldest son by his first marriage, Major Lawrence Washington and half-brother of George, who married Annie, oldest daughter of William Fairfax of Belvoir.

The mill was built by Washington's father, and in the old house, as shown near to it, he and Mary the mother may have been domiciled while for four years they were living on the Hunting Creek plantation. The youthful George was then under ten years of age. The family removed from the locality to Fredericksburg in 1739 or 1740. Seven years later, at the close of his school-days, George returned to live with his elder brother Lawrence, who had built for himself the middle or main portion of the present Mount Vernon house.

WASHINGTON'S SERVANTS.

JUST before the war it was not uncommon to read in the newspapers the announcement of the death of "another of Washington's Servants." Then almost every octogenarian darkey in "Old Fawfax" claimed to have belonged to "Mars Joge," and could tell wonderful stories of old times at Mount Vernon. But of late no mention has been made of these worthies. All of them have passed over the borders and joined the ranks of the plantation armies beyond. In this connection we cannot refrain from giving to the reader the ballad of "Thornton Gray," one of "de old sarvants" whom the writer once interviewed, and who was reputed to have been an offshoot of African royalty.

He was an ancient colored man,
His age one hundred ten;
He hailed from old Virginy,
And once a slave had been.

His hair was thin and silver'd,
　His brow with furrows set,
Features fine cut and moulded,
　And face as black as jet.

In olden times, the story ran,
　That kings and noblemen,
In Afric's sultry climate,
　His forefathers had been ;

And as I gazed upon him,
　And closely scann'd his mien,
It seemed a trace of royalty
　Full well might yet be seen.

He bow'd him low and tip'd his hat,
　And laid aside his hoe,
The while I briefly interview'd
　About the long ago.

" My name is Thornton Gray," he said ;
　" Dey calls me ' Uncle Thorn,'
Lived mos'ly in Old Fairfax,
　In Wes'mo'land was born.

" Was ris by Mars' Wilkers'n,
　Great farmer, may depend ;
Own'd all de big plantation
　Dey call'd de ' River Bend.'

" Made heaps of fine tabacca,
　Had stores of corn and wheat ;
Hard labor, mind you ; but de han's
　Had plenty den to eat.

" Times ain't de same as den dey was,
　'Pears like dey's chang'd all round,
De folks dat lived when I was young,
　All dead and under ground.

" 'Taint long I knows for me to stay,
Here　There after all de res';
I only waits de Lord's good time,
　Sho'ly he knows de bes'.

" I soon shall yhear de trumpeter
　Blow on his trumpet horn,
An' call me home to glory,
　An' de riserickshum morn,"

My good freed man, to him I said,
　Of age, one hundred ten,
You might relate much history
　Of former times and men.

I wait to hear the story,
　Which none can tell but you,
For none have lived fivescore of years
　And ten more added to.

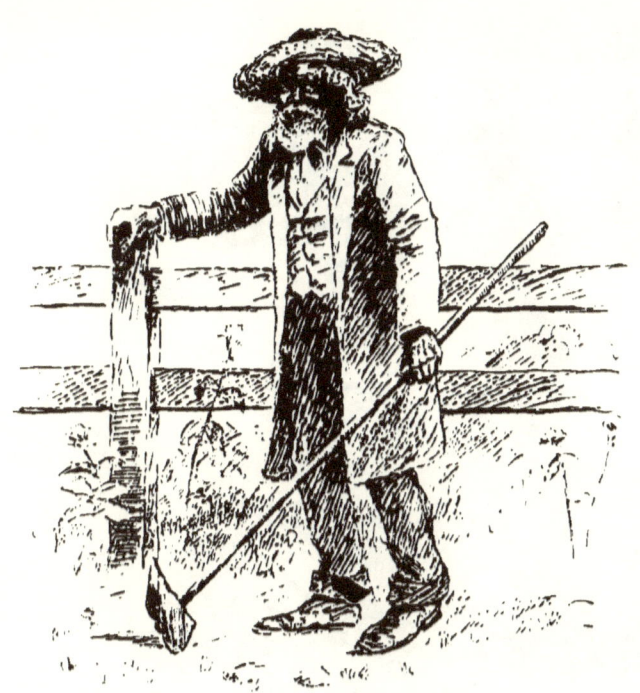

THORNTON GRAY, ONE OF WASHINGTON'S "SARVINTS."

(Page 41.)

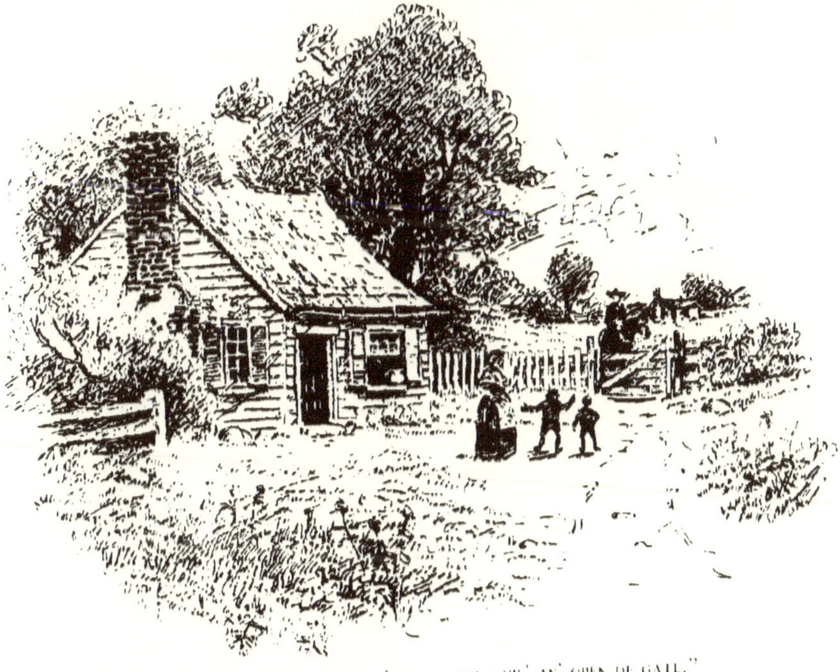

"DAR COM' MARS' GEOG' WASH'NTON. RUN CHIL' AN' OPEN DE GATE."

(Page 42.)

POHICK CHURCH IN THE OLDEN TIME.

You must have seen the Britishers,
And heard the cannons roar;
" Why, bless you, chil', was mos' a man,
And heard and seen de war."

And Washington, you must have seen,
That great and good hero
Who led the Continentalers,
And fought our battles through!

" Why surely I has seen him,
And know'd him well; for, boss,
I was de Gineral's sarvant,
Took care de Gineral's hoss!

" Fine man he was for sartin,
Good friend to all de poor—
Dar's none in dese days like him,
And none, folks said, before."

Enough, I said! I'm well repaid;
And grasped his trembling hand—
No honor hath a man like this,
In all our glorious land!

No further did I question him
About the long ago,
And when I said to him good-bye,
He took his garden hoe.

Who hath beheld our Washington,
And lived to tell us so,
Deserves as well a story
As many others do.

And hence our homely ballad,
A tribute slight to pay
To this departed colored man,
And ancient—Thornton Gray.

OLD POHICK CHURCH.

FIVE miles below the Mount Vernon mansion, and three miles from the Potomac, stands the old Pohick Church edifice, erected in the year 1772. It was built from plans furnished by Washington, who was a member of its vestry, and a frequent attendant at its services. The eccentric Mason L. Weems, author of a life of Washington, and also a life of Marion, and who was as ready to tune a fiddle as to preach a sermon, was one of its rectors before 1800. The picture represents an old-time congregation after service.

THE PASSING AWAY OF WASHINGTON.

" How sleep the brave who sink to rest
With all their country's honors blest."

THERE came to Mount Vernon a bleak, forbidding winter day,
December 13, 1799. Washington was engaged in planning and
superintending some improvements on his estate which occupied his
presence till a late hour in the evening, when, on returning to the
mansion, he complained of cold and a sore throat, having been wet
through by mists and chilling rain. He passed the night with
feverish excitement, and his ailment increased in intensity during
the next day and until midnight, when, surrounded by his sorrowing
household and the medical attendant, he passed gently and serenely
from the scenes of earth to the realities of the great unknown. He
was in the sixty-eighth year of his age. His faculties were strong and
unimpaired to the last. He was conscious from the first of his malady,
that his end was near, and he awaited the issue with great composure
and self-possession. " I am going," he observed to those around him.
" But I have no fears." His mission had been well and nobly
accomplished. His great life-work, whose influences will reach to the
remotest periods of time, was accomplished.

At the supreme moment Mrs. Washington sat in silent grief at his
bedside. " Is he gone?" she asked in a firm and collected voice.
The physician, unable to speak, gave a silent signal of assent. " 'Tis
well," she added in the same untremulous utterance; "all is over
now. I shall soon follow him; I have no more trials to pass through."
She followed three years later. They both rest side by side in the new
burial vault at the old homestead by the river.

The following quaint announcements of Washington's death from
the newspapers of this locality will be of interest :

The Georgetown *Centinel of Liberty*, a semi-weekly, in its issue of
December 17, 1799, thus announces Washington's death : " It is our
painful duty first to announce to the country and the world the death
of General George Washington. This mournful event occurred on
Saturday evening about eleven o'clock. On the preceding night he was
attacked with a violent inflammatory affection of the throat, which in
less than twenty-four hours put a period to his life. If a long life
devoted to the most important public services; if the most eminent
usefulness, true greatness, and consummate glory : if being an honor
to our race and a model to future ages : if all these could rationally
suppress our grief, never perhaps ought we to mourn *so little*. But as
they are the most powerful motives to gratitude, attachment, and veneration · for the living and of sorrow at their departure, never ought
America and the world to mourn more than on this melancholy
occasion."

The *Alexandria Times* and District of Columbia *Advertiser*, of
Friday, December 20, 1799, of which one-half sheet is all that is
known to be in existence, thus announced Washington's death and
funeral : " The effect of the sudden news of his death upon the inhabi-

tants of Alexandria can better be conceived than expressed. At first a general disorder, wildness, and consternation pervaded the town. The tale appeared as an illusory dream, as the raving of a sickly imagination. But these impressions soon gave place to sensations of the most poignant sorrow and extreme regret. On Monday and Wednesday the stores were all closed and all business suspended, as if each family had lost its father. From the time of his death to the time of his interment the bells continued to toll, the shipping in the harbor wore their colors half-mast high, and every public expression of grief was observed. On Wednesday, the inhabitants of the town, of the county, and the adjacent parts of Maryland proceeded to Mount Vernon to perform the last offices to the body of their illustrious neighbor. All the military within a considerable distance and three Masonic lodges were present. The concourse of people was immense. Till the time of interment the corpse was placed on the portico fronting the river, that every citizen might have an opportunity of taking a last farewell of the departed benefactor.''

WASHINGTON'S BIRTHDAY AND BIRTHNIGHT BALL.—February 22, 1732.

> What day is this of proud acclaim,
>   Of rolling drum and trumpet strain,
> And banners floating on the breeze,
>   And cannon booming loud again?
>
> A people come with grateful praise,
>   And hearts in unison,
> As well befits to celebrate
>   The birth of Washington!
>
> From East and West and North and South,
>   Throughout our broad domain,
> The plaudits of a nation swell
>   O'er mountain, hill, and plain.
>
> Not for ambition's selfish deeds—
>   Not for the conq'ror's name,
> This day the glorious meed is given,
>   But for the nobler fame,
>
> By man world wide accorded
>   And grander grown by time—
> The fame that comes of duty
>   And life of deeds sublime.

AT the close of the Revolution commenced the birthday celebrations and birthnight balls in honor of the successful chief. They soon became general all over the republic. The first of these was held in Alexandria.

In the large cities where public balls were customary, the birthnight ball in the olden time was the gala assembly of the season, and was attended by an array of fashion and beauty.

The first President always attended on the birthnight. The etiquette was not to open the festivities until the arrival of him in whose honor it was given; but so remarkable was the punctuality of Washington in all his engagements, whether for business or pleasure, that he was never waited for a moment in appointments for either.

The minuet, now obsolete, for the graceful and elegant dancing of which Washington was conspicuous, in the vice-regal days of Lord Botetort in Virginia, declined after the Revolution. The commander-in-chief danced for his last time a minuet in 1781 at the ball given in Fredericksburg in honor of the French and American officers on their return from the triumphs of Yorktown. The last birthnight he attended was in Alexandria, February 22, 1798. He always appeared to enjoy the gay and festive scenes of those occasion, remaining till a late hour with the participants, his neighbors and friends; for, remarkable as he was for reserve, and the dignified gravity inseparable from his nature, he ever looked with most kind and favoring eye upon the rational and elegant pleasures of life.

WASHINGTON'S HABITS, MANNERS, AND APPEARANCE.

THE work which Washington accomplished in the course of his public and private duties was simply immense. And when we estimate the volume of his official papers,—his vast foreign, public, and private correspondence,—we can scarcely believe that the space of one man's life could have comprehended the performance of so many varied things. But he brought order, method; and rigid system to help him. These accessories he relied on, and they led him successfully through. He rose early. His toilet was soon made. A single servant prepared his clothes and laid them in readiness. He shaved and dressed himself, but gave very little of his precious time to matters of that sort, though remarkable for the neatness and propriety of his apparel. His clothes were made after the old-fashioned cut, of the best though of the plainest materials. The style of his household and equipage when President corresponded with the dignity of his exalted station. About sunrise he invariably visited and inspected his stables. Then he betook himself to his library till the hour of breakfast. This meal was plain and simple, and with but little change, from time to time. Indian cakes, honey, and tea formed this temperate repast. On rising from the table, if there were guests, and it was seldom otherwise, books and papers were offered for their amusements, and requesting them to take care of themselves the illustrious farmer proceeded to his daily tour over his farms. He rode over them unattended, opening the gates, letting down and putting up bars as he visited his laborers, and inspected their operations. He was a progressive farmer and introduced many new methods in the tillage of his lands. His afternoon was usually devoted to his library. At night his labors over, he would join his family and friends at the tea-table and enjoy their society for several hours, and about nine o'clock retired to bed. When without company he frequently read aloud to his family circle from newspapers and entertaining books.

Washington liked the cheerful converse of the social board. After his retirement from public life, all the time he could spare from his library was devoted to the improvement of his estate and the elegant and tasteful arrangement of his house and grounds. The awe that was felt by every one upon the first approach to Washington evidences the imposing power and sublimity which belongs to real greatness. Even the frequenters of the courts of princes were sensible of this exalted feeling when in the presence of the hero, who, formed for the highest destinies, bore an impress from nature which declared him to be one among the noblest of her works.

Washington at the age of forty-three was appointed commander-in-chief. In stature he a little exceeded six feet; his limbs were sinewy and well-proportioned : his chest broad; his figure stately, blending dignity of presence with ease. His robust constitution had been tried and invigorated by his early life in the wilderness, his habit of occupation out-of-doors, and his rigid temperance ; so that few equalled him in strength of arm or power of endurance. His complexion was florid ; his hair dark brown ; his head in its shape perfectly round. His broad nostrils seemed formed to give expression and escape to scornful anger. His dark blue eyes, which were deeply set, had an expression of resignation, and an earnestness that was almost sadness.

THE FIRST CELEBRATION OF THE ADOPTION OF THE FEDERAL CONSTITUTION.

IT is remarkable that the first report of a celebration in Alexandria in any way connected with national affairs was reported by no less a hand than that of General George Washington. When the news reached that city that the requisite nine States had acceded to the Federal Constitution, the people of Alexandria immediately ordered a festival, and Washington, after attending it, addressed his friend, Charles Pinckney, under date of Mount Vernon, June 28, 1788, as follows :

"No sooner had the citizens of Alexandria, who are Federal to a man, received the intelligence by the mail last night, than they determined to devote the day to festivity. But their exhilaration was greatly increased, and a much keener zest given to their enjoyments, by the arrival of an express, two hours before day, with the news that the Convention of New Hampshire had, on the 21st instant, acceded to the new confederacy by a majority of eleven voices. Thus the citizens of Alexandria when convened constituted the first assembly in America who had the pleasure of pouring a libation to the prosperity of the ten States which had already adopted the general government ;" and, after speculating upon the course of the remaining States, he added : "I have just returned from assisting at the entertainment." These citizens had a dinner at the City Hotel, which is still standing.

A SUMMARY OF WASHINGTON.

Nobles are made by patents,
Which kings and queens bestow,—
Of such the names of thousands,
The books of lineage show.

But only nature's patent
Can give the noble aim,
To true nobility of purpose,
She only gives the claim.

GEORGE WASHINGTON, whether as a private citizen, mingling
with his neighbors and friends in a social or business capacity,
or whether as a dignified actor and director in the public and national
affairs of his country, is one of the very few men in the records of
history who have successfully and triumphantly withstood the test
and scrutiny of the world's adverse criticism.   He stands out on the
shifting scenes of the world's annals as a grandly imposing and unique
personage, meriting and commanding as well, the veneration of every
observer, no matter of what country or nationality,—and the citizens
of the country he loved and defended, in their enthusiasm and gratitude for his brilliant public services, love to contemplate him as a
personage divinely ordained and appointed to open the way, not only
for civil and religious liberty in America, but everywhere among the
oppressed of humanity.

He was not a soldier because of his fondness for tinsel, parade, or
mere military glory, but because of the exigencies of the times in
which he lived.   After these exigencies had passed, he gladly yielded
up all investiture of military authority and dropped back to the enjoyment of the calm delights of peace and quietude in his rural retreat,
not sighing, as many a warrior had done before him, that there were
no more campaigns to direct, no more victories to achieve, but rejoicing in the coming of the blessed reign of peace.   His mission as
a soldier had been grandly accomplished, and he was well content to
await its beneficent results.

As a victor he was magnanimous, lenient, and forbearing—never
vaunted of his military prowess; and of all the pictorial representa-
tions which adorned his rooms at Mount Vernon, not one of them
represented any of the revolutionary scenes in which he had figured.

There have been soldiers who have achieved mightier victories in
the field, and made conquests more nearly corresponding to the bound-
lessness of selfish ambition ; statesmen who have been connected with
more startling upheavals of society ; but it is the greatness of Washington, that in public trusts he used power solely for the public good ;
that he was the life, and moderator, and stay of the most momentous
revolution in human affairs; its moving impulse and its restraining
power.   Combining the centripetal and the centrifugal forces in their
utmost strength, and in perfect relations, with creative grandeur of
instinct, he held ruin in check, and renewed and perfected the institu-
tions of his country.   Finding the colonies disconnected and dependent,
he left them such a united and well-ordered commonwealth as no
visionary had believed to be possible.   So that it has been truly said,
"he was as fortunate as great and good."   This also is the praise

of Washington, that never in the tide of time has any man lived who had in so great a degree the almost divine faculty to command the confidence of his fellow-men and rule the willing. Wherever he became known, in his family, his neighborhood, his county, his native State, the continent, the camp, civil life, the United States, among the common people, in foreign courts, throughout the civilized world of the human race, and even among the savages, he, beyond all other men, had the confidence of his kind."

On the sixteenth of June, 1775, he appeared in his place in Congress, after his appointment as commander-in-chief of the colonial armies, and after refusing all pay beyond his expenses, he spoke with unfeigned modesty to his colleagues,—"As the Congress desire it, I will enter upon the momentous duty, and exert every power I possess in their service and for the support of the glorious cause. But I beg it may be remembered by every gentleman in the room that I this day declare, with the utmost sincerity, I do not think myself equal to the command I am honored with."

Washington was not a bigot nor a zealot in religion, nor even a sectarian. "Profoundly impressed with confidence in God's providence, and exemplary in his respect for the forms of public worship, no philosopher of the eighteenth century was more firm in the support of freedom of religious opinion; but belief in God and trust in His overruling power formed the essence of his character. He believed that wisdom not only illumines the spirit, but inspires the will. He was a man of action, and not of theory or words. His creed appears in his life, not in his professions. His whole being was one continued act of faith in the eternal, intelligent, moral order of the universe. His broad and liberal conceptions of what constituted the basis of a common fatherhood and a common brotherhood would not allow of any narrowing or dwarfing of his natural convictions by the trammels of religious dogmas or formulas, and so he was tolerant of the fullest religious liberty and thought, believing that every man had the right implanted in him by the God of nature to worship Him in whatever way seemed to him best, consequently the creed of no church ever held him exclusively within its narrow limits. His true and tried friends were confined to no religious denomination, but were chosen from the widest range of religious thought, and selected only for real worth and integrity of character. As his diary bears witness, he was accustomed to attendance at all forms of worship, and doubtless he always found something in each which his unprejudiced judgment could approve and accept. In his neighborhood no churches existed but the Episcopal. These the laws of the colony had established, to the prejudice of all others, and made respectable, and it was quite natural, from his reverential and orderly habits, that he should have been a habitual attendant at their services with his neighbors; and while he was one of the vestry in the church of both Alexandria and Pohick, he doubtless busied himself very little about vestry matters, further than to fill the numerical requirements." *

* In those times the duties of the church vestry embraced not only religious matters but also many secular neighborhood affairs, requiring the judgment of just such a practical man as Washington.

He appears to have been so impressed with the importance of listening to the inward monitor, or, as the Quakers are wont to express
it, "the still, small voice," that in his rules of civility and behavior,
written out by him for his guidance at the age of thirteen, he enjoined
upon himself "to labor to keep alive in his breast that little spark of
celestial fire called conscience." At that early age his code of rules
show that he had determined to begin life right, and the story of all
his subsequent years is evidence that he continued right. The germs
of innate goodness and excellence had been implanted in his being,
and, through wise parental solicitude and instruction and a strict
obedience to duty, they steadily and beautifully unfolded to public
observation and admiration with the passing of the years of his life.
The pole-star of his impulses and the drift of his being were right
and duty; to these everything was subordinate. He read correctly
the motives of men and measured accurately their capabilities, and
rarely erred in his estimate of character. He was frank in his intercourse,—never dissembled, never stooped to mean devices or subter-
fuges. While he was open and courteous, fraternal and approachable,
he was never trivial, never forgot his dignity, but always, whatever
the occasion, so demeaned himself as to inspire every one with whom
he came into contact, whether socially or in a business way, with the
feeling that he was one of the very first of men among men. He was
not an orator, and seldom attempted to express himself at length on
any public occasion, but as a writer he excelled. His style, as preserved in many volumes of miscellaneous letters and state papers, was
plain, clear, and without unnecessary verbiage, and his expressions
were rarely marred by instances of false syntax, though he had never
had the advantages of more than a very limited common school education; but from his youth upward he had been a constant and attentive reader of the best literature of the times, and was very observant
of acknowledged models of the English language.

In all his business transactions, and they were many and varied, no
instance has been recorded by any writer of any attempt on his part
to get the advantage of any of his fellows. He was a fast friend and
a patron of merit. He recognized the divinity of labor, and believed that it should be respected and fully requited. True, he was a
slave-holder, but it was for the reason that labor was urgently needed
in those times to open and subdue the wilderness, produce supplies,
and develop the great resources of the country; but he did not look
upon his bondsmen as mere machines, devoid of feelings or sensibilities. There is the most authentic evidence that he looked most
carefully after their welfare in respect to diet, raiment, quarters, and
seasons of toil; had them taught habits of industry, provided medical
attendance for them in sickness, allowed them religious instruction,
and by his last bequest, made July 9, 1799, ordered that they should
all be freed. And it is but just to mention in this connection that
from no one of his freed folks or their immediate descendants has
there ever been heard any instance of unnecessary severities under his
benign rule as a master.

The estate was large and land for tillage was plenty, and every family had ample privileges of having plots of ground for growing all kinds of vegetables, while fish were abundant in the river and creeks, and wild game plenty in the woods.

In 1786, he wrote to Robert Morris, "There is not a man living who wishes more sincerely than I do to see a plan adopted for the abolition of slavery. But there is only one proper and effectual mode by which it can be accomplished, and that is by legislative authority : and this, as far as my suffrage will go, shall never be wanting." And in another letter, written to his nephew, Robert Lewis, August 17, 1799, four months before his death, he says, " I have more negroes on my estate of Mount Vernon than can be employed to any advantage in the farming system ; and I shall never turn planter thereon. To sell the overplus I cannot, because I am principled against that kind of traffic in the human species. To hire them out is almost as bad, because they cannot be disposed of in families to any advantage ; and to disperse the families I have an aversion."

In a letter to John F. Mercer, of Virginia, September, 1786, he wrote, " I never mean, unless some particular circumstances should compel me to it, to possess another slave by purchase, it being among my first wishes to see some plan adopted by which slavery in this country may be abolished by law." Martha, his widow, in 1801, manumitted all the slaves she held in her own right.

The relation of the African race to our nation, Washington represented. He was not a radical reformer, not an ideal theorist, but a practical thinker and actor, and as such, he interpreted the African's destiny. He recognized his capacity to be a tiller of the soil and a mechanic, and treated him kindly ; and taught and practised the principle of emancipation. He regarded slavery, indeed, as the law of the land, and denied the right of any citizen to interfere with the legal claims of the master to his slave, but he thought the law ought to be changed, and he stands in our history as the representative of the old school of emancipationists who regarded slavery as a fading relic of a semi-civilized form of society. He could work with the negro and mingle praise with blame in his judgments, and, without having extreme opinions of their gifts or virtues, he thought them fitted for freedom and capable of education.

He was methodical in all his undertakings and pursuits, no matter of how commonplace. Kept a diary of ordinary as well as extraordinary events, and noted down regularly from day to day his expenditures, whether incurred for household necessities, raiment, the carrying on of his farm arrangements, or for travelling. His handwriting, from his characteristic order and care, was invariably neat and legible, whether he wrote a state paper, a letter to some home or foreign dignitary, or whether he wrote a deed for the conveyance of land, or an order on his merchant, or a receipt to his mechanic, every letter was well formed and distinct, so that it never required, as is too often the case with public men, much time to decipher his meaning.

As a farmer, he was not content to merely follow the modes which had long prevailed with the planters around him, but at a very early period of his farming operations he put into practice new and more

advantageous systems of cropping and manuring ; laid down his land
to grass ; planted out orchards of the best fruits then obtainable ;
employed the newest agricultural implements, and had a constant care
to obtain the best seeds and the most improved stock.   Washington
was a farmer by choice and because he believed the " calling to be the
most healthful, the most useful, and the noblest employment of man."
He might have entered many avenues opened for him when a young
man which would have led him to distinction, for he had that within
him which would have insured success whatever the undertaking.   But
the quietude and peaceful surroundings of a rural life were more in
keeping with his natural inclinations than the circumstances of other
pursuits, which to many of the young men now coming up around us
seem far more attractive.

He was domestic in his habits, and loved the peace, the tranquillity,
and joys of home life.   And we most delight to dwell on the part of
the history of this great man which pictures that life—the life he led
as a plain, unpretending citizen of the republic he had been so instrumental in establishing.   What to a man of the finer sensibilities is the
tinselry and show and power of a public life when compared with
genial minds and with nature clothed in the simple and beautiful garb
of truth ?   Of all men, none could appreciate the difference better than
Washington.   " I am now, I believe," he writes in a letter from
Mount Vernon, " fixed in this seat, and I hope to find more happiness in retirement than I ever experienced in the wide and bustling
world."

His hospitality was large, and his generosities and charities wide-
reaching.   No one was more ready to acknowledge an error of heart
or judgment, nor more magnanimous to those differing in opinions.

We do not claim that he was perfect, for perfection in humanity is
impossible.   We only claim for him that he came as near to filling the
measure of the " noblest work of God" as any other man in history.
And certainly no character in all its aspects or bearings is more
worthy of emulation by the youth of our country than his.   His
closing scene on the fourteenth of December, 1799, was peaceful, and
a grateful people mourned for him as a father indeed.

GUNSTON—THE HOME OF GEORGE MASON.

'Twas an old colonial palace,
    Ere that brazen boom
Thunder'd freedom from the State House
    Thro' the thrilling land.
In those days it was a great house,
    Spacious, feudal, grand.

THE next place of historic interest below Belvoir is Gunston, an
    estate once containing seven thousand acres, the home of
George Mason, who is known in history as the author of Virginia's
Bill of Rights and her Constitution ; and who served as one of her
earlier governors.   He came of a distinguished and honored English

Yr. most obd: Sert

G Mason

stock. He was fifth in descent from that George Mason, the first of
the family in Virginia, who was a member of the British Parliament
in the reign of Charles I., and who opposed with eloquence the arbi-
trary measures of the king, but at the commencement of the civil
war drew his sword in his favor against the soldiers of Cromwell, and
afterwards commanded a regiment under Charles II. at the battle of
Worcester, and later, in disguise escaped to Virginia, the refuge of
many distinguished royalists, and landed in the county of Norfolk in
1651. Comparatively little has been written of the career of the
George Mason of our sketch. It lives rather in tradition than in the
pages of history. Such a fact is unworthy of his countrymen. He
married Ann Eilbeck, of Charles County, Maryland, who died at the
age of thirty-nine. After many years he married a lady of the name
of Brent, but of this union there was no issue. He was one of the
best and purest men of his time, and possessed the confidence of
those younger civilians, Jefferson, Madison, and Monroe, whose opinions he did much to mould and shape along the lines which led to
American independence. He was a near neighbor to Washington
and the Fairfaxes, and on the most intimate terms with them. In
1776 we find him writing to his agent in London a powerful statement of the wrongs inflicted by the mother government upon the
colonies; and about the same time appeared his masterly exposition
of "colonial rights," entitled "Extracts from the Virginia charters,
with remarks upon them." In 1769 he drafted the " Articles of
Association" against importing British goods, which the Burgesses
signed in a body on their dissolution by Lord Botetourt; and in
1774 he drew up the celebrated Fairfax County Resolutions, upon the
attitude to be assumed by Virginia. In 1776 he was elected to represent his county in the convention of that year, and drew up the " Bill
of Rights" already alluded to, which was adopted. Jefferson, then in
Philadelphia, had written "a preamble and sketch" to be offered; but
Mason's had been reported, and the final vote was about to be taken
when it arrived. Mason's bill was therefore adopted, but Jefferson's
" preamble" was attached to the Constitution. Mason sat afterwards
in the Assembly, and supported Jefferson in his great reforms of the
organic laws, as the cutting off of entails, the abolishing of primo-
geniture, and the overthrow of church establishments. The disinterested public spirit of the man may be inferred from the fact that, by
birth and education, he belonged to the dominant class and to the
Episcopal Church. He also advocated the bill forbidding the further
importation of slaves in 1778, and ten years afterwards sat in the Convention to decide on the adoption or rejection of the Federal Constitution. He was elected one of the senators for Virginia, but declined
the honor on account of pressing home duties. He continued to reside on his Gunston estate, contented and happy, though suffering at
times from attacks of gout, an hereditary enemy. His death occurred
in 1792, at the age of sixty-six, and his remains, unmarked by stone
or tablet, rest in the Gunston family burial-place, but in the much
admired group of sculptured heroes and statesmen which adorns State
House Square in Richmond his statue is conspicuous.

Such is a brief outline of the life of a remarkable man, whose services to his State were almost inestimable. He was deficient in powers of oratory; but, like Jefferson, who shared the same disability, was all powerful with the pen. The "Bill of Rights" will live longer than the eloquence of Patrick Henry, however, for it stands as it was written, while the utterances of the great prophet of the Revolution are even now fading from the memories of men. The "Bill of Rights" is enough to perpetuate the fame of its author in the absence of all other memorials of his life. It is a great and masterly statement of constitutional rights, and remains to-day, as it ever will, the corner-stone of republican government. Derived in a measure from Mason's long and profound study of the great writers of England upon constitutional freedom, it was yet, in the comprehensive sense, entirely original, for he infused into it the free spirit of the New World. From all the great and noble men who were then prominent in public affairs, the Fairfax County planter was selected to perform this important work, and the fact is an incontestable proof of the favorable light in which his contemporaries regarded the character of his mind and his genius.

In social life George Mason showed to great advantage. Though somewhat stately and formal in his bearing, no man was more engaging in deportment towards his friends, and no friends were warmer than his own. In person he was rather above the medium height, full in form, and with a courtly and erect figure. His statue represents him correctly,—in full court dress, with ample ruffles, and looking composedly and serenely forward. It is the look of a man who "knows his rights," and, "knowing, dare maintain," whatever dangers stand in the path or threaten his vindication of them. Few of our people are aware of how much of our republican faith has come down to us from George Mason and his Virginia company, wrought out in the stormy days of the Revolution.

The Gunston estate is separated from Belvoir by Accotink Bay. It has been divided and subdivided since the time of its distinguished proprietor into many small farms, now mostly owned and occupied by Northern settlers. The mansion, built in the year 1739 by the subject of our sketch, is one of the very few types of the best order of houses of the early colonial days which have escaped the ravages of time and the brand of the incendiary. Its massive, well-cemented walls of bricks brought from Old England by tobacco ships, and its interior structures of wainscoting and panelling, and other work of the joiner, have continued through the many generations almost intact. Gunston Hall was built after the old manor-house of the Mason family in England. It is about eighty feet in length by forty in width, and is a more pretentious structure than that of Mount Vernon. The old-fashioned wide hall and the spacious parlors are carved tastefully and minutely. In the year 1742 there was shipped from the landing of this estate twenty-two thousand bushels of wheat and five large cargoes of tobacco, packed in the old-fashioned hogsheads.

Gunston has furnished three United States senators and several members of Congress; and after Mount Vernon is, without doubt, the

GUNSTON HALL.

most historic home in Virginia. The following lines were written by
a sojourner under its roof on a Christmas night a few years ago :

I sat in Gunston Hall ;—
Grim shadows on the wall
　Around me pressed,
As memories of the past
Came crowding thick and fast,
And to my mind, at last,
　　Their theme addressed.

Back from the shadowy land
They pressed, a noble band,
　A stalwart race ;—
I saw them come and go,
As if they thought to show
Their stately grandeur to
　My mind apace.

From wall and ceiling high,
And ancient panel nigh,
　Their faces showed ;
I marked them, one and all,
Majestic, grand, and tall,
As from the corniced wall
　Their shadows strode.

Then hall and mansion wide
They filled on every side,
　With phantoms grand ;
While, at the outer gate,
Pressed carriages of state,
With spectral steeds to mate
　The shadowy band.

I saw the hearth-stones blaze,
As in colonial days,
　At this old hall ;
With beauty flashing high,
And gallants thronging nigh,
As if some love-lit eye
　Held them in thrall.

They seemed to grow apace
Like old Antenor's race,
　Of Trojan fame ;
Or men of lofty state,
On whom the good and great
Bestowed their utmost weight
　Of honored name.

Then prouder forms were seen,
Of more majestic mien,—
　Those grand old knights,
Whose sires at Runnymede　•
Stocked England with a breed
Of men that made kings heed
　Their subjects' rights.

Their spectral grandeur showed
In every step they trode
    Through ancient hall,
While women held their place
Supreme in every grace
With which the Gothic race
    Invests them all.

Each captive husband vied,
With lover by his side,
    To own her sway,
Who practised less the art
To win than keep a heart
That once to Cupid's dart
    Had fallen prey!

While wives with sweethearts strove
To keep the torch of love
    In constant flame,
That, like sweet Omphale,
They might retain their sway,
And yet their lords obey
    By rightful claim.

So passed the shadowy throng,
In misty group along,
    As fancy played,
Or pictured, one by one,
These spectral scenes upon
My mind, as night wore on
    With deep'ning shade.

And as my eyelids fell
They grew more palpable—
    These spectres grand,
That still, in Gunston Hall,
Hold nightly carnival,
As fancy stirs withal
    Her conjurer's wand.

The eldest son of George Mason the fifth, the subject of our sketch, was George of "Lexington," a captain in the Revolutionary Army, and succeeded his father at his death, in 1792, to the possession of Gunston Hall, and was the last of the name that ever lived there. He left five sons and four daughters, all of whom married and had issue. The fourth and last surviving son was John Mason, of Analastan Island, the father of James Murray Mason, who was from 1847 to 1861 United States Senator from Virginia.

With Slidell he figured in the Trent affair, and was afterwards Confederate commissioner in England. He was the only direct descendant ever in the upper house of Congress.

The eldest daughter of John Mason became the wife of the late Samuel Cooper, formerly in the Federal service, and afterwards Adjutant-General of the Confederate Army. Another daughter married S. Smith Lee, brother of Robert E. Lee, and was the mother of Governor Fitzhugh Lee.

THE INAUGURATION OF WASHINGTON.

"IT would seem, from all we have learned of Washington's early and later career, that Providence had specially appointed him by birth and education to be the leader and director in the Western world of the revolution which was to open the way for the founding there of a new and a free English-speaking nation. Every factor, whether of lineage or culture, in his admirably balanced character as well as every aspiration of his heart from his cradle to his grave is of exceeding great interest to the world. Although deprived of a father's care at the age of eleven years, he was, however, especially blest in having such a mother as the noble Mary Washington, who conscientiously discharged her sacred duty as his guardian, counsellor, and friend. Hence, filial reverence grew with his growth and strengthened with his maturing years into fixed principles, making him throughout all his eventful life loyal to every virtue and heroic in every trust. He seems to have had no idle boy life, but was a man with manly instincts and ambitions from his youth."

There came a sunshiny day in April, 1789, when George Washington, President-elect of the United States by the unanimous voice of the people, stood on a balcony in front of the Senate Chamber in the old Federal Hall on Wall Street, to take the oath of office. An immense multitude filled the streets and the windows and roofs of the adjoining houses.

Clad in a suit of dark brown cloth of American manufacture, with hair powdered, and with white silk stockings, silver shoe-buckles, and steel-hilted dress sword, the hero who had led the colonies to their independence came modestly forward to take up the burdens that peace had brought. Profound silence fell upon the multitude as Washington responded solemnly to the reading of the oath of office, "I swear—so help me, God."

Then, amid cheers, the display of flags, and the ringing of all the bells in the city, our first President turned to face the duties his countrymen had imposed upon him. In sight of those who would have made an idol of him, Washington's first act was to seek the aid of other strength than his own. In the calm sunshine of that April afternoon, fragrant with the presence of seed-time and the promise of harvest, we leave him on his knees in Old St. Paul's, bowed with the simplicity of a child at the feet of the Supreme Ruler of the universe.

MARY, THE MOTHER.

YOU have reared this beautiful obelisk to one who was "the light of the dwelling" in a plain rural colonial home. Her history hovers around it. She was wife, mother, and widow. She nursed a hero at her breast. At her knee she trained to the love and fear of God and to the kingly virtues, honor, truth, and valor, the lion of the tribe that gave to America liberty and independence. This is her title to renown. It is enough.

Eternal dignity and heavenly grace dwell upon the brow of this blessed mother; nor burnished gold nor sculptured stone nor rhythmic praise could add one jot or tittle to her chaste glory. She was simply a private citizen. No sovereign's crown rested on her brow. She did not lead an army, like Joan of Arc, or slay a tyrant, like Charlotte Corday. She was not versed in letters or in arts. She was not an angel of mercy, like Florence Nightingale, nor the consort of a hero, like the mother of Napoleon. But for the light that streamed from the deeds of him she bore, we would doubtless have never heard the name of Mary Washington, and the grass that grew upon this grave had not been disturbed by curious footsteps or reverential hands. —*Daniel's Oration.*

MARY WASHINGTON.

THE Rappahannock ran in the reign of good Queen Anne,
　All townless from the mountains to the sea,
Old Jamestown was forlorn and King Williamsburg scarce born —
'Twas the year of Blenheim's victory,
Whose trumpets died away in far Virginia
　On the cabin of an old tobacco farm,
Where a planter's little wife to a little girl gave life,
　And the fire in the chimney made it warm.

It was little Mary Ball, and she had no fame at all,
　But the world was all the same as if she had;
For she had the right to breathe and to tottle and to teethe,
　And to love some other cunning little lad:
Though he proved a widower, it was all the same to her,
　For he gave her many a daughter and a son,
And the family was large and the oldest, little George,
　Was the hope of little Widow Washington.

The name resounded not in the time we have forgot,
　It was nothing more than Smith or Jones or Ball;
And George's big half-brothers had the call on their stepmother's
　Affection, like the babes of her own stall;
They paid the larger taxes, and the Ayletts and Fairfaxes
　Received them in their families and lands,
While the widow thought upon it, she rode in her sunbonnet,
　Midst her slaves who tilled her gulleys and her sands.

Till they sought to take her George upon the royal barge,
　And give him a commission and a crest,
When her heart cried out, " O, no!   Something says he must not go;
　My first-born is a father to the rest."
She could find him little schooling, but he did not learn much fooling,
　And he dragged the mountains o'er with chain and rod,
The Blue Ridge was his cover and the Indian his lover
　And his Duty was his Sovereign and God.

Still her rival in his heart was the military art,
　And the epaulettes she dreaded still were there.
There are households still where glory is a broken-hearted story,
　And the drum is a mockery and snare.
From the far-off Barbadoes, from the yell of Frenchmen foes,
　From the ghost of Braddock's unavailing strife,
She beheld her boy return and his bridal candles burn,
　And a widow like herself became his wife.

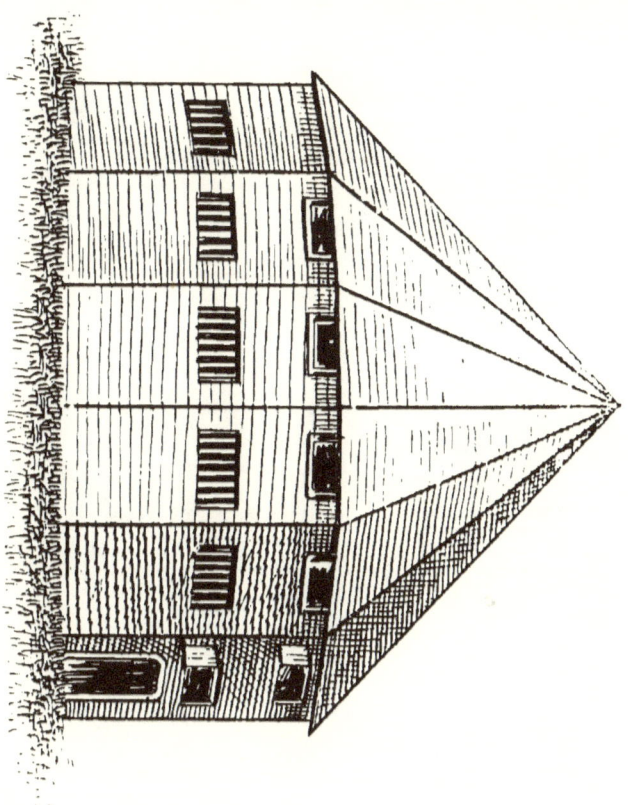

WASHINGTON'S SIXTEEN-SIDED BARN.

By Potomac's pleasant tide he was settled with his bride,
  Overseeing horses, hounds and cocks and wards,
And it seemed but second nature to go to the legislature
  And play his hand at politics and cards.
Threescore and ten had come when the widow heard the drum,
  " My God !" she cried, " what demon is at large ?"
'Tis the conflict with the king, 'tis two worlds a mustering,
  And the call of Duty comes to mother's George.

" O war ! To plague me so ! Must my first-born ever go ?"
  Her answer is the bugle and the gun.
The town fills up again with the horse of Mercer's men,
  And the name they call aloud is Washington.
In the long, distracting years none may count the widow's tears :
  She is banished o'er the mountains from her farm ;
She is old and lives with strangers, while ride wide the king's red rangers,
  And the only word is " Arm !" and " Arm !" and " Arm !"

" Come home and see your son, the immortal Washington,
  He has beat the king and mighty Cornwallis !"
They crowd her little door and she sees her boy once more ;
  But there is no glory in him like his kiss.
The marquises and dukes, in their orders and perukes,
  The aides-de-camp, the generals and all,
Stand by to see and listen how her aged eyes will glisten
  To hear from him the tale of Yorktown's fall.

Upon that her lips are dumb to the trumpet and the drum ;
  All their pageantry is vanity and stuff.
So he leans upon her breast she cares nothing for the rest—
  It is he and that is victory enough !
In the life that mothers give is their thirst that man shall live
  And the species never lose the legacy.
To love again on earth and repeat the wondrous birth—
  That is glory—that is immortality.

Unto Fredericksburg at last, when her fourscore years are past,
  Now gray himself, he rides all night to say :
" Madame—mother—ere I went to become the President
  I have come to kiss you till another day."
" No, George ; the sight of thee, which I can hardly see,
  Is all for all—good-by ; I can be brave.
Fulfil your great career as I have fulfilled my sphere ;
  My station can be nothing but the grave."

The mother's love sank down, and its sunset on his crown
  Shone like the dying beams of perfect day ;
He has none like her to mix in the draught of politics
  The balm that softens injury away.
But he was his mother's son till his weary race was done ;
  Her gravity, her peace, her golden mien
Shed on the state the good of her sterling womanhood,
  And like her own was George's closing scene.
                              George Alfred Townsend.

WASHINGTON'S BARN.

WASHINGTON had an inventive as well as a systematic and
  thorough turn of mind, and was always devising some new
and better method for the lessening of the labors of the hands on his
estate. He greatly improved many of the unwieldy implements then

in use, such as ploughs, harrows, hoes, and axes ; for he had carpenter, smith, and smithy always at hand to materialize his ideas.

His circular, or sixteen-sided, barn of brick and frame, sixty feet in diameter, with two stories, was the wonder of his neighbors. The threshing or treading-out floor, ten feet wide, was in the second story, all round the centre mows ; and the oxen or horses were taken up to it by an inclined plane. The floor of it was of open slats, that the grains might, without the straw, fall through to the floor below. Later, he had constructed a device, worked by horse-power, by which the heads of wheat sheaves, held on a table against rapidly-revolving arms, were beaten out ; and was probably the first step, after the hoof and flail, towards the power-thresher of the present day.

WASHINGTON'S COACH.

MADE in England, 1789. The body and wheels were of cream color, then very fashionable, with gilt relief, and the body was suspended upon the old-fashioned, heavy, leathern straps, like those of the former-day stage-coaches. Part of the sides and front were shaded by green Venetian blinds, enclosed by black leather curtains. The lining was of black, glossy leather. The Washington arms were handsomely painted on the doors, with the characteristic motto, " *Exitus, acta probat,*"—the result proves actions. Upon each of the four panels of the coach was a picture of the four seasons. Usually, the General drove but four horses, but on going from Mount Vernon to the seat of government, at Philadelphia or New York, he drove six.

DESCENT OF MOUNT VERNON.

JUDGE BUSHROD WASHINGTON, who inherited Mount Vernon from his uncle, General Washington, was the third child of John Augustine Washington and his wife Hannah, daughter of Colonel John Bushrod, of Westmoreland County, Va. He came into full possession of the estate after the demise of Mrs. Martha Washington, widow of the general, which occurred May 22, 1802. Judge Washington was a Justice of the Supreme Court of the United States, and resided at Mount Vernon, dispensing a liberal hospitality, and keeping intact his inherited landed estate to the time of his death. He was married in 1785 to Anna, daughter of Colonel Thomas Blackburn, of Rippon Lodge, Prince William County, Va. They had no children. He made a will, and, following the example of his illustrious uncle, he provided for his wife during her life and then disposed of his estate to his nephews and nieces, giving specific directions, and leaving the mansion house and the Mount Vernon farm proper, with restricted bounds, which he specifically defined, to his nephew, John Augustine Washington, from whom the Ladies' Association purchased.

∧ father of the John A. Washington,

EXTRACTS FROM WASHINGTON'S DIARY.

1774.

WENT to Pohick Church with Mr. Custis.
Went to the barbecue at Accotink.
Colonel Pendleton, Mr. Henry, and Colonel Mason came in the evening and stayed all night.

Colonel Pendleton, Mr. Henry, and I set out on our journey to Philadelphia to attend the Congress.

Dined with Mr. Pleasants (a Quaker).

Dined with Joseph Pemberton (a Quaker).

Went to Quaker meeting in the forenoon, and to St. Peter's in the afternoon.

Went to Christ Church, and dined at the New Tavern.

Went to the Presbyterian meeting in the forenoon, and to the Romish church in the afternoon.

Went to Christ Church in the afternoon.

Dined at the New Tavern with the Pennsylvania Assembly, and went to the Ball afterwards.

1773.

May 1. Went fishing in Broad Creek.

April 13, 1774. In company with Colonel Bassett went fishing in Broad Creek.

A LOVE SONNET OF WASHINGTON AT THE AGE OF SIXTEEN, FROM HIS DIARY.

OH ye gods, why should my poor resistless heart
    Stand to oppose thy might and power,
At last surrender to Cupid's feather'd dart,
    And now lays bleeding every hour
For her that's pitiless of my grief and woes,
    And will not on me pity take.
He sleeps amongst my most inveterate foes,
    And with gladness never wish to wake.
In deluding sleepings let my eyelids close,
    That in an enraptured dream I may
In a soft, lulling sleep and gentle repose
    Possess those joys denied by day,
From your bright, sparkling eyes I was undone ;
Rays you have ; more transparent than the sun,
Amidst its glory in the rising day
None can you equal in your bright array ;
Constant in your calm and unspotted mind ;
Equal to all, but will to none prove kind.
So knowing, seldom one so young, you'll find.
Ah ! woe's me, that I should love and conceal,
Long have I wish'd, but never dare reveal,
Even though severely love's pains I feel :
Xerxes that great, wast free from Cupid's dart,
And all the greatest heroes felt the smart.

A LOVE LETTER WRITTEN AT SIXTEEN, FROM HIS DIARY.

DEAR SALLY,—This comes to Fredericksburg fair in hopes of meeting with a speedy passage to you if your not there, which hope you'l get shortly, altho I am almost discouraged from writing to you, as this is my fourth to you since I received any from yourself. I hope you'l not make the old proverb good, out of sight out of mind, as its one of the greatest pleasures I can yet forsee of having in Fairfax, in often hearing from you, hope you'l not deny me.

I pass the time much more agreeably than what I imagined I should, as there's a very agreeable young lady lives in the same house where I reside (Colonel George Fairfax's wife's sister), that in a great measure cheats my sorrow and dejectedness, tho not so as to draw my thoughts altogether from your parts. I could wish to be with you down there with all my heart, but as a thing almost impracticable shall rest myself where I am with hopes of shortly having some minutes of your transactions in your parts which will be very welcomely received by your

GEO. W.

COLONEL WASHINGTON, OF MOUNT VERNON.

OWING to the death, some years before, of Lawrence Washington's only child, Sarah, followed as it shortly after was by that of his widow Annie, Colonel George Washington, already proprietor of the paternal estate on the Rappahannock, had inherited, with much additional property, the magnificent domain of Mount Vernon, and was now one of the wealthiest planters of the Old Dominion. Washington's fondness for agricultural pursuits had not been the only motive of his retirement. The harassing cares of his command had not exerted a complete monopoly of his thoughts during this prolonged period of Indian warfare. The romantic traditions of his courtship it is unnecessary to recall here. On the seventeenth of January, 1759, he was married to Mrs. Custis, a very young and wealthy widow, who formerly had been the most attractive belle at the vice-regal court of Williamsburg. The ceremony was performed, amid a joyous assemblage of relatives and friends, at the White House, the bride's home, where they remained until the trees were budding at Mount Vernon, when they took up their permanent residence there. Washington at this time wrote to a friend, "I am now, I believe, fixed in this seat, with an agreeable partner for life, and I hope to find more happiness in retirement than I ever experienced in the wide and bustling world. . . . . No estate in America is more pleasantly situated. In a high and healthy country; in a latitude between the extremes of heat and cold; on one of the finest rivers in the world—a river well stocked with various kinds of fish at all seasons of the year. The borders of the estate are washed by more than ten miles of tidewater. The whole shore is one entire fishery." The whole region thereabout, with its range of forests and hills and picturesque promontories, afforded sport of various kinds, and was a noble hunting-ground.

These were, as yet, the aristocratical days of Virginia. The estates were large, and continued in the same families by entail. A style of living prevailed which has long since faded away. The houses, liberal in all their appointments, were fitted to cope with the free-handed, open-hearted hospitality of the owners. Each estate was a little empire, and its mansion-house the seat of government, where the planter ruled supreme. The negro quarters formed a hamlet apart. Among the slaves were artificers of all kinds, so that a plantation produced within itself everything for ordinary use. Articles of fashion and elegance, luxuries and expensive clothing were imported from London, for the planters on the Potomac carried on an immediate trade with England. Their tobacco, put up by their own negroes, bore their own marks, and was shipped directly to their agents in Liverpool or Bristol. But have not all these things been chronicled in the annals of the house of Castlewood?

Washington, instead of trusting to overseers, gave his personal attention to every detail of the management of his estate. He carried into his rural affairs the same method, activity, and circumspection that had distinguished him in military life. He made a complete survey of his lands, apportioned them into farms, and regulated the cultivation of all. The products of his estate became so noted for the faithfulness—as to quality and quantity—with which they were put up, that it is stated that any barrel of flour that bore the brand of George Washington, Mount Vernon, was exempted from the customary inspection in the ports to which it was sent. There were many relaxations in the arduous duties he had assumed. He delighted in the chase. In the height of the season he would be out with the fox hounds two or three times a week, accompanied by his guests and the gentlemen of the neighborhood, and ending the day with a hunting dinner, when he is said to have enjoyed himself with unwonted hilarity. He also greatly relished duck-shooting, in which he was celebrated for his skill. The Potomac was the scene of considerable aquatic state at that time, and Washington had his barge, rowed by six uniformed negroes, to visit his friends on the Maryland side of the river. He had his chariot and four, with black postilions in livery, for the use of Mrs. Washington and her lady visitors. As for himself he always appeared on horseback. His stable was well filled and admirably regulated—his stud all thoroughbred. Occasionally he and Mrs. Washington would pay a visit to Annapolis, and partake of the gaieties which prevailed during the sessions of the legislature.

In this round of rural occupation, rural amusements, and social intercourse, Washington passed many tranquil years, the halcyon season of his life. His already established reputation drew many visitors to Mount Vernon, who were sure to be received with cordial hospitality. His marriage was unblessed with children, but those of Mrs. Washington received from him parental care and affection. His domestic concerns were never permitted to interfere with his public duties. As judge of the county court, and member of the House of

Burgesses, he had numerous calls upon his time and thoughts; for whatever trust he undertook, he was sure to fulfil with scrupulous exactness.

THE COMMANDER-IN-CHIEF.

The storm of the Revolution, so long impending, had suddenly burst over the land, and Washington, who had represented Virginia in the First Continental Congress, and was now a member of the second, was by it, June 15, 1775, unanimously called to the command of the colonial army. On the 20th he received his commission, and the following day started for Boston on horseback to take command. "There is something charming to me in the conduct of Washington," wrote John Adams at the time. "A gentleman of one of the first fortunes on the continent, leaving his delicious retirement, his family and friends, sacrificing his ease and hazarding all in the cause of his country. His views are noble and disinterested." And Mrs. Adams wrote on his arrival before Boston, "Dignity, ease, and complacency, the gentleman and the soldier, are agreeably blended in him. Modesty marks every feature of his face." The honors with which he was received only told him how much was expected from him, and when he looked around upon the raw and rustic levies he was to command, "a mixed multitude of people, without discipline, order, or government," scattered about in rough encampments, beleaguering a city garrisoned by an army of veteran troops, with ships of war in its harbor, he felt the awful responsibility of his situation, and the complicated and stupendous task before him. "The cause of my country," he wrote, "has called me to an active and dangerous duty, *but I trust that Divine Providence will enable me to discharge it with fidelity and success.*" With what unswerving and untiring fidelity, and with what complete and splendid ultimate success—despite disaster, mutiny, faithlessness, and treachery in those most trusted, privations without parallel, difficulties such as never leaders encountered before, bitter rivalries, the opposition of Congress, and the loss of confidence, as once wellnigh seemed, of a whole people—Washington, never faltering, discharged his trust during the long, weary years that followed needs no repetition here. There are no better known pages in the world's history.

AT MOUNT VERNON AGAIN.

Having resigned his commission to the Congress at Annapolis (December 23, 1783), Washington hastened to his beloved Mount Vernon, arriving on Christmas Eve in a frame of mind well suited to enjoy the festival. "I feel now," he wrote, "as I conceive a weary traveller must do, who, after treading many a weary step with a heavy burden on his shoulders, is eased of the labor, having reached the haven to which all the former were directed." And again: "The scene is at last closed. I am now a private citizen on the banks of the Potomac. I feel myself eased of a load of public care. With heartfelt satisfaction will I tread the paths of private life; and this being the order of my life, I will move gently down the stream of life until I sleep with my fathers." Throughout the whole of his campaigns he had kept himself informed of the course of rural affairs at Mount Vernon. By means of maps, on which every field was laid down and numbered, he was enabled to give minute directions as to their cultivation. Now he gladly resumed the direct management. His diaries show how diligently he improved the groves and shrubbery about the house. At the opening of the year he transplanted ivy under the walls of the garden (to which it still clings), planted hemlock trees, and sowed holly berries in a semicircle around the lawn, many of the bushes from which flourish in full vigor now. Each day's labor was noted down—how he went in quest of young elms, ash trees, white thorn crab-apples, mulberries, willows and lilacs, laid out winding walks and planted trees and shrubs along them ; how he sowed acorns and buckeye nuts brought from the Monongahela, opened vistas through the pine grove, and twined around his columns scarlet honeysuckles, to blossom all the summer. His careworn spirit freshened up in these employments. With him Mount Vernon was a perpetual idyl. The transient glow of poetical feeling which once visited his bosom when in boyhood he rhymed beneath its groves seemed about to return once more, and we please ourselves with noting among the trees set out by him a group of young horse chestnuts from Westmoreland, the home of his childhood, sent to him by the son of his "Lowland Beauty."

ENLARGEMENT OF THE MANSION.

Washington made no change in the appearance of the mansion (as left by his brother) until 1785, when he determined to enlarge it, in order to provide for the increasing number of his guests. He obtained from England workmen and materials, and by the close of this year had completed his improvement, in which he was his own architect, drawing every plan and specification with his own hand. The interior of the old house remained unchanged ; but wings were added and the exterior remodelled. Its appearance to-day is as when completed then. It was of the most substantial frame-work (cut in imitation of stone), two stories and attic in height, ninety-six feet in length by thirty in depth, with a piazza fifteen feet in depth extending along the entire eastern or river front, supported by square columns twenty-five feet in height, over this a light balustrade, and in the centre of the roof an observatory and spire. There were seven high dormer windows—three on the eastern side, one on each end, and two on the western or lawn side. The ground floor contained six rooms (there were originally but four), with the old spacious hall in the centre of the building, extending through it from east to west, and the stairway. On the south side of the hall was the parlor, library, and breakfast-room, from which last a narrow staircase ascended to the private study on the second floor ; on the north side a music-room, parlor, and dancing-room, in which when there was much company the guests sometimes entertained at table. The principal feature of this room was the large mantelpiece, wrought in Italy, of statuary and Sienite

5

marbles, exquisitely carved in every part, bearing in relief scenes in agricultural life. The interiors of the new rooms were finished to correspond with the old ones. At the same time were built, near the mansion, on either side, a substantial kitchen and laundry, connected with it by colonnades. These, with other outlying buildings there erected, all remain, with the exception of an extensive conservatory. Washington, thus occupied with the development of his estate, was meanwhile unconsciously exercising a powerful influence on national affairs. He was obliged to maintain an extensive correspondence, and the opinions and counsels given in his letters were widely effective. No longer the soldier, he was now becoming the statesman.

THE FIRST PRESIDENT.

The electors chosen under the new Constitution were unanimous in calling Washington to the presidential chair. On the 16th of April, 1789, he again bade adieu to Mount Vernon, and set out for the seat of government. His progress to New York was a continuous ovation. There on April 30 the first President of the United States was inaugurated.

It is not our purpose to dwell upon the incidents of the following eight years, when Washington so worthily filled the loftiest position within the gift of any people. During this period, crowded with events most important in the formative history of the republic, its chief magistrate—it may surprise those unfamiliar with the publications of the time—was pursued in his official acts, and even private life, by a bitter partisan malignity, the like of which is almost unknown in our later day. The pressure of public duties admitted but few opportunities to visit his home. During one of these visits there, in the summer of 1796, he wrote his farewell address, which a great British historian has declared to be "unequalled by any composition of uninspired wisdom." He was now looking forward with unfeigned longing to his retirement. His term of office expired March 4, 1797, when Mr. Adams, in his inaugural address, spoke of his predecessor as one "who, by a long course of great actions, regulated by prudence, justice, temperance, and fortitude, had merited the gratitude of his fellow-citizens, commanded the highest praises of foreign nations, and secured immortal glory with posterity."

THE HAVEN OF REST.

He was now at Mount Vernon again, to the repose of which he had so often turned a wistful eye throughout his agitated and anxious life. The opening spring caused the rural beauties of the place to exert for him all their sweetening influences. His mansion required repair, and he wrote : "I am already surrounded by joiners, masons, and painters, and such is my anxiety to be out of their hands that I have scarcely a room to put a friend into, or to sit in myself, without the music of hammers and the odoriferous scent of paint." To another friend : "My hours glide smoothly on. The repair of my buildings and cultivation of my farms will occupy the few years I may be a sojourner here." And so it was. Surrounded by an affectionate family, entertaining troops of friends, engaged in the most fascinating of all pursuits, truly his " lines were cast in pleasant places." To this tranquil life there was but one transient interruption, when, in view of the impending war with France, he was called (July 3, 1798) yet again into the public service as Commander-in-Chief of all the American armies, and immediately repaired to Philadelphia, where, in the work of organization, he remained until the danger was happily averted, when he returned to Mount Vernon, never more to leave it.

IMPROVEMENT AND PROTECTION OF THE MOUNT VERNON ESTATE.

ELSEWHERE in this "Hand-Book" allusion has been made to the changes which have been wrought on the Mount Vernon Estate since the passing away of its distinguished proprietor at the close of the last century. First, of its rapid decadence, through neglect and improvident culture, from well ordered conditions of agriculture to those of unthrift and desolation, and finally, after the lapse of half a century, of the coming of new hands from places remote, to begin the work of transforming the wasted areas to fields of waving grain and clover, and to orchards of abundant fruitage. The work of restoration has been increasing from year to year since 1852, and, now that the electric railway has made the entire domain suburban to Alexandria and Washington, the prospect of still greater improvements becomes brighter and more encouraging. With the cheap and rapid transit which will be afforded by this road to and from these cities there will doubtless be large accessions of new settlers from localities far less favored, to occupy the divisions and subdivisions of the many large farms of the estate.

Just after the Mexican war, when the general government was casting about to find a suitable location for the National Military Asylum, or Soldiers' Home, as it is now called, the Hon. Lewis McKensie and other prominent citizens of Alexandria proposed and strenuously urged upon the authorities the acquirement by purchase of a thousand acres of the estate for that purpose. No more fitting choice could have been made for a soldier's refuge, and the property could have been secured at that time for less than thirty thousand dollars.

In 1859, the "Ladies' Association," with their patriotic contributions of two hundred thousand dollars, purchased the "Mansion" and two hundred acres, and began the work of restoring and preserving the buildings and the immediate grounds. How well they have succeeded in their efforts, the present attractive appearance of the premises and the orderly arrangement of policing and other daily duties incident to the reception of visitors most satisfactorily attest. But there is a rapidly increasing conviction, nevertheless, among all such as reverence the name and goodly fame of Washington all over our land, that the time has come for the control of the " Home and Tomb" to pass into the hands of the general government, that our people may be relieved from the odium of laying all pilgrims to this much frequented shrine under capitation tribute before allowing them permission to enter the gates of its enclosures. As Washington was above and beyond all merely mercenary motives, and despised undignified schemings, so the place which was honored by his living presence and which holds his ashes ought to be accessible without money or price. In Europe every mausoleum of note is freely opened to visitors without charge, and not only every mausoleum but every depository of arts and literature; and reproachful allusions are not unfrequently heard by American tourists abroad from foreigners who have been required to pay a fee at the entrance to the mausoleum of George Washington.

May we not hope that among the many unreasonable customs of our country which are doomed to pass away before the march of progress, this discreditable custom of levying tribute at the gates of Mount Vernon may be among the first to be discontinued. To the objection so often urged by those who look with disfavor upon the change proposed, that the place under government control would not be so well cared for and guarded from depredations as under the present provident management of the ladies, it seems only necessary to refer to the result through many years of that control of the Smithsonian and national museums, the agricultural grounds, and public parks, the Congressional library and other public charges now under exclusive government care. A tithe of the yearly appropriations wasted on worthless fortifications and warships would amply suffice to keep up all needed repairs at Mt. Vernon, and a small detail of soldiers from the army would supply the required work of policing and protect all from the hands of the spoiler.

THE "PRINCETON" CATASTROPHE; BURSTING OF THE "PEACEMAKER."

ON the 28th of February, 1844, a large party of ladies and gentlemen of Washington city, including President Tyler and the members of his Cabinet with their families, were invited by Commodore Stockton, of the navy, to pass the day on board the frigate "Princeton," lying at anchor off the city of Alexandria. The day was fine and the company numerous and brilliant, not fewer than four hundred in number, of whom the majority were ladies. After the arrival of the guests, the "Princeton" got under way and proceeded down the river to a short distance below Fort Washington. During the passage down, the largest gun of the vessel, the "Peacemaker," carrying a ball of two hundred and twenty-five pounds, was fired several times to test its strength and capacity. The gun had been constructed from a model of, and under the immediate direction of, the commodore, and Mr. Tyler had manifested a great interest in its success. At two P.M. the ladies of the party were invited to a sumptuous repast in the cabin. The gentlemen succeeded them at table, and some of them had got through and left it. The ship was on her return to her anchorage, and when opposite to Broad Bay, the commodore proposed, for the special gratification of the President and his Cabinet, to fire the gun again, a salute, as he said, in honor of the "great peacemaker" of his country—George Washington. Accordingly, all the members of the Cabinet started to go up-stairs, the President with them, but at that instant they were called back to hear a toast proposed by Miss Wicklife. It was this: "The flag of the United States, the only thing American that will bear a stripe." This was received with great enthusiasm. The President in response then gave as a toast, " the three great guns,—the " Princeton," her commander, and his " Peacemaker." This was loudly applauded by the ladies, and then the members of the Cabinet started to go up-stairs again. At this moment, Mr. Upshur, of Virginia, Secretary of State, had his hand on the President's arm, and said to him, " Come, Mr. Tyler, let's go up and see the gun fired." Just then Colonel Dade asked Mr. Waller, the President's son-in-law, to sing an old song about 1776. The President replied, " No, by George, Upshur, I must stay and hear that song ; it's an old favorite of mine. You go up, and I'll join you directly." Accordingly, away went Upshur, Gilmer, and the others to see the gun fired. Messrs. Benton, Phelps, Hannegan, Jarnegan, Virgil Maxey, Commodore Kennon, Colonel Gardiner, and many others following. The President remained below listening to the singing, and just as Mr. Waller came to the name of Washington off went the gun. "There," said the master of ceremonies, " that's in honor of the name, and now for three cheers." And just as they were about to give them, a boatswain's mate rushed into the cabin begrimed with powder and said that the " big gun" had exploded and killed many of those on deck. On this announcement the shrieks and agonizing cries of the women were heart-rending,—all calling for their husbands, fathers, brothers, and so on, rushing wildly into their arms and fainting with excess of feeling. When the gun was fired the whole ship shook, and a dense cloud of smoke enveloped the entire group on the forecastle, but when this blew away an awful scene presented itself to the spectator.

The lower part of the gun, from the trunnions to the breech, was blown off, and one-half section of it was lying on Mr. Upshur. It took two sailors to remove it. Mr. Upshur was badly cut over the eye and on his legs; his clothes were literally torn from his body. He expired in about three minutes. Governor Gilmer, of Virginia, was found to be equally badly injured. He had evidently been struck by the section of the gun before it had reached Mr. Upshur. Mr. Sykes, member of Congress from New Jersey, endeavored to raise him from the floor, but was unable. A mattress was brought for him, but he soon expired. Mr. Maxey, of Maryland, had his arms and one of his legs cut off, the pieces of flesh hanging to his mutilated limbs, cold and bloodless, in a manner truly frightful. He died instantly. Mr. Gardiner, ex-member of New York, and Commodore Kennon, lingered about half an hour, unconscious, and expired without a groan. The flags of the Union were placed over the dead bodies as their winding sheets. Behind the gun, the scene, though at first equally distressing, was less alarming. Commodore Stockton, who was knocked down, almost instantly rose to his feet and jumped on to the wooden carriage to survey the effects of the calamity. All the hair of his head and face was burnt off. Judge Phelps, of Vermont, had his hat blown off. Nine seamen were seriously wounded and Colonel Benton and many others were stunned by the explosion. Such was the force of it that the starboard and larboard bulwarks of the ship were shattered and the gun blown into many pieces.

Judge Wilkins had taken his stand by the side of Governor Gilmer, but some remarks falling from the lips of the latter, and perceiving that the gun was about to be fired he exclaimed, "Though Secretary of War, I don't like this firing, and believe that I shall run," so saying he retreated, suiting the action to the word, and escaped injury. The most heart-rending scene, however, was that which followed. The two daughters of Mr. Gardiner, of New York, were both on board and lamenting the death of their father, while Mrs. Gilmer, from whom they in vain attempted to keep the dreadful news of the death of her husband, presented truly a spectacle fit to be depicted by a tragedian. There she sat on deck, with hair dishevelled, pale as death, struggling with her feelings, and with the dignity of a woman, her lips quivering, her eyes fixed and upturned without a tear, soliloquising, "Oh, certainly not! Mr. Gilmer cannot be dead! Who would dare to injure him? Yes, O Lord, have mercy upon me! O Lord, have mercy upon him!" And then, still more apparently calm and seeming to be collected, with the furies tearing her heart within, "I beseech you, gentlemen, to tell me where my husband is! Oh! impossible, impossible! and he, can he, can he be dead? Impossible." Here Mr. Senator Rives, of Virginia, drew near. "Come near, Mr. Rives," she said in a soft whisper, which resembled Ophelia's madness, "tell me where my husband is—tell me if he is dead. Now certainly, Mr. Rives, this is impossible." Mr. Rives stood speechless, the tears trickling down his cheeks. "I tell you, Mr. Rives, it is impossible," she almost screeched; and then again moderating her voice, "Now do tell his wife if her husband lives!" Here several ladies exclaimed, "God grant that she may be able to cry; it would relieve her"—"if not, she must die of a broken heart."

A daughter of Mr. Gardiner, one of the victims of the ill-fated party, and to whom the President was paying attention, and who in the following June became his wife, gave the following relation a few years ago. "When we got down to the collation served in the cabin, the President seated me at the head of the table with him and handed me a glass of champagne. My father was standing just back of my chair, so I handed the glass over my shoulder, saying, 'Here, pa.' He did not take it, but said, 'My time will come.' He meant his 'time to be served,' but the words have always seemed to me prophetic. That moment some one called down to the President to come and see the last shot fired, but he replied that he could not go, as he was better engaged. My father started with some other gentlemen and left us. Just then we heard the report, and the smoke began to come down the companion-way. 'Something must be wrong,' I said to a bystander, who started to go and see. He got to the door, then turned around and gave me such a look of horror, that I never shall forget it. That moment I heard some one say, 'The Secretary of State is dead.' I was frightened, of course, and tried to get up stairs. 'Something dreadful has happened,' I exclaimed. 'Let me go to my father!' I cried, but they kept me back. Some one told me the gun had exploded, but that there was such a crowd around the scene it would be useless for me to try to get there. I said that my father was there, and that I must know if any evil had befallen him. Then they told me he had been wounded. That drove me frantic. I begged them to let me go and help him—that he loved me, and would want me near him. A lady, seeing my agony, said to me, ' My dear child, you can do no good ; your father is in heaven.' ''

The bodies of the victims of this dire calamity, which cast a gloom over the whole land, were taken up to the Capital. Five hearses, conveying the remains of Messrs Upshur, Gilmer, Kennon, Maxey, and Gardiner, followed by a long train of carriages and a great concourse of citizens, on horseback and afoot, passed in silence up Pennsylvania Avenue and proceeded to the Executive Mansion. The coffins of the distinguished dead were taken into the East Room and placed on biers to await the funeral solemnities which occurred on the Saturday following.